Behind
the
Wall

by

ROBERT E. A. LEE

WM. B. EERDMANS PUBLISHING CO., GRAND RAPIDS, MICH.

for Elaine

IN THAT STATE OF SUSPENSION BETWEEN THE END OF HIS NIGHT'S sleep and the opening of his eyes to mid-morning, he lay on the bed and slowly became aware of the rhythm of the sounds coming through his open window. His room faced on Clayallee, one of West Berlin's busiest thoroughfares. He knew the sounds — the peculiar engine patter of the diesel Mercedes, the impatient cylinder staccato of speeding Volkswagens, the whining whistle of motorbikes, the heavy-duty rumble of U. S. Army trucks, and the coughing of transit busses.

He opened his eyes to the new day. His mother had been in his room earlier and had laid out for him fresh underwear and a newly pressed shirt. On the table by his bed there was a little vase of garden flowers, picked that morning. How she loved to fuss over him. It was a perfect arrangement for her that he had decided to spend his holidays in Berlin. She would, of course, have coffee and breakfast waiting for him and, as soon as she knew that he was awake, she would devote herself to serving him.

How wonderful to be home again! For a moment or two, while automatically following the routine of getting out his shaving things, he almost believed it — that this was his home. He smiled to himself in the mirror as he considered the unlikelihood of a grand Berlin mansion like this being his home or the home of his family. His mother was the housekeeper here, and he felt at home with her while the family she served summered in Switzerland.

"Werner dear, good morning!" his mother called from downstairs. "Did you sleep well?"

"Morning, Mother! Like a baby! Did you try to wake me? I slept longer than I thought I would."

"But you are on vacation — why should I wake you? I set your breakfast out on the sun porch. Would you like an egg?"

"Thanks, no. Just coffee and bread."

It was more comfortable with sunglasses out on the veranda. The sun was very bright and it was a perfect day in every way. As his mother brought in the pot of steaming coffee, pride and happiness glowed on her face.

"Good appetite, Werner darling," she said as she bent down to kiss him lightly on the cheek.

"Sit down, Mother. Today this is your home, and my home too. You might as well enjoy it. Have a cup of coffee with me."

"Oh, that would be nice. Let me get another cup — and your mail. I almost forgot, there are some letters for you." She brought him two letters from Hamburg. One was a business envelope, obviously a communication from his office. The other surprised him more. It was a blue envelope addressed in the delicate hand of a woman.

He left the envelopes unopened on the table. He looked up at his mother and could see that she was curious to know about the life he was leading in Hamburg. She would wonder about the letter from Gertrude. He wondered about it too, because they had decided that they were not right for each other after all, and they had said good-by. He really wished that she had not written to him; that only complicated things. He was already beginning to enjoy a kind of freedom that would allow him to look at another girl without a guilty conscience. And it made quite a difference. Last night he had been in East Berlin, and had met a girl who somehow

8

fascinated him. He was hoping he might see her again today. But he was not quite ready to share all this with his mother.

"What are your plans for today, Werner?"

Should he tell her that he planned to go over to East Berlin again? She was not aware that he had been there last night. He would have liked to take her over sometime, but of course no resident of West Berlin was allowed to go across. Fortunately his own residence was now officially Hamburg and West Germans like himself still had the opportunity to go to East Berlin.

"I thought I'd go over to East Berlin this afternoon." He decided to mention it without talking about last night. "I'd like to drive around and see how things have changed in the last year. I might drive over to Mügelsee."

"Could you try to see your Uncle Klaus?" his mother beamed. "I haven't seen my brother, you know, since the Wall. Perhaps I could send some fruit over, or some coffee, or even some tobacco and a letter. I will write a letter to him if you could deliver it."

"Sure, why not? I'd enjoy talking with him again. But no coffee or cigarettes. They're not allowed. The control police might search my car. The fruit would be okay and I can have some extra smokes for him in my pockets."

His mother immediately went to make preparations and to write a letter to her brother in East Berlin, thinking about the days before the Wall. Before the Wall they had seen each other every week end. It had been specially comforting for her to have him in Berlin because her husband had died six years earlier. She was a lonesome woman, with her children scattered all over the world. Heinz was in Brazil, Clara in Italy, and Margretha in Munich. Werner was the closest, in Hamburg. It was almost unbelievable that she could have him with her in this house. Her own son — for a whole month.

Sipping the last of his coffee, he slit open the blue envelope:

Dear Werner, Forgive me for writing to you. I know that we had said good-by and that was to be the end of it. I do not mean to start it again as I think we agreed it was for the best. But I felt I had to tell you at least that I am not angry, that I won't be bitter. I will remember our friendship and our love, and will always think well of you, Werner. I hope you will think well of me also. Perhaps we can meet sometime. And when we do, we can look each other in the eyes and know that we are still friends and hold a kind of respect between us. That is all I wanted to say, except also to say thank you for — well, thank you for your friendship. Yours, Gertrude.

Had he and Gertrude done the right thing? He thought about their talk and how they had agreed to part and how he had felt happy over the result. It was right that they should go their separate ways. But why did she have to send this letter and remind him again? He stuffed the letter into his pocket, still a little annoyed that she had written.

He forgot the blue envelope and Gertrude as he jumped into his Volkswagen, shoved the sliding roof back to catch the sun, and started down Clayallee, the broad Berlin boulevard that curved along the periphery of the Grunewald section. As he drove by the United States Military Mission Headquarters buildings, he caught a glimpse of the Stars and Stripes at the entrance. This flag gave him a feeling of security. Most West Berliners, he thought, did not resent the occupying power. They knew that if the Americans and the British and the French would leave, West Berlin could not survive the circling Red pressures of Soviet Germany.

Now he saw three U.S. Army tanks coming down Clayallee towards him and he shuddered even though he also instinctively recognized them as a symbol of West Berlin's security. His memories of the war, even as a little boy, still gave him sleepless nights, and military tanks were brutal vehicles of death and destruction that haunted him often.

He pointed his Volkswagen toward Kurfürstendamm. The streets were familiar, and yet so many things were new that it seemed almost like some other town, some other German city. Even with all the evidence of booming prosperity and construction in sight, he felt that a miracle like this could not really happen. There was virtually no trace of the unbelievable chaos, rubble, and destruction of the hellish nightmare that was 1945. *The war did not really happen,* he said to himself. *The old Berlin is somewhere else. This is a modern city, prosperous, busy, and happy. The city of Berlin has been resurrected from the dead!*

But then, down on Kurfürstendamm, that vibrant and lively street, he saw a grim, ghastly reminder that the war did happen. The old skeleton of the Kaiser Wilhelm Church stood out defiantly in crazy juxtaposition to the starkly modern new church building of concrete and glass, the two structures declaring the inescapable tension between what was and what is.

And then there was the Wall to contend with. Before August 13, 1961, he would have followed the traffic over to the *Avenue of June 17* toward the Brandenburg Gate, to that street whose name would forever memorialize the 1953 uprising in East Berlin and East Germany. It might have succeeded had it not been crushed by Russian tanks. But today there was the ugly Wall in front of the Brandenburg Gate and Werner could not pass through.

Dropping his deeper reflections for the moment, he remembered to turn south. Checkpoint Charlie was not for him, but only for non-German civilians, the Allied forces in Berlin, and diplomatic personnel. He would have to find Heinrich-Heinstrasse, the special break in the Wall where West Germans could pass. There was no thoroughfare leading directly to it. He had to turn down one street and then another before he found the crossing point. Apparently others had found it before him because there was a line of about ten cars waiting.

He turned off the engine of his Volkswagen and got out of the car to look at the lineup ahead of him. Although a U.S. Military Police car was parked to one side, West Berlin police seemed to be in charge. Over one store near the checkpoint he saw a sign: *Freedom must not end here!*

With exasperating slowness — a few yards every five or six minutes — the cars moved ahead. Finally he was asked to show his identification to the officer on duty — his passport as a citizen of the Federal Republic of Germany. Address: Hamburg. The registration for his car: HH 4327, which the officer immediately recognized as a vehicle from *Hansestadt Hamburg*. While he waited, several sight-seeing busses came through and went to the head of the line. He saw them squeeze their way through the amazingly narrow opening in the cement-block Wall. Before anyone could reach the opening, two metal barriers had to be lifted by the Vopos from the East on duty. He noticed that these policemen in the green uniform of the Volkspolizei were very young in their late teens or early twenties. They must have gone through careful screening to have this assignment so close to West Berlin. After all, hadn't other Vopos on duty here before them defected? Some 350 uniformed men had made a dash for freedom through the Wall since it had been built.

When he finally got through to the other side of the Wall, additional obstacles remained for him. The government of the East had a long building for passport control and customs clearance. He was directed to park his Volkswagen along one side. Before getting out of the car, he took a pack of cigarettes from his pocket and tossed it on the seat of the car. The Vopos who searched his car later would know what that meant and would probably give him an easier time if they recognized him on another visit.

He took his place at the end of the line of weary tourists, businessmen, children, parents and grandparents waiting to go over. He stood in line for twenty minutes. Over to his left he watched a man and a boy on the East side waving a

12

white handkerchief in the direction of some person standing behind the barriers on the West side. He wondered what kind of communication without words they could have at that distance. Perhaps just the communication of sight, simply knowing that the other was there and was recognized. A Wall and a world separated the two.

"May I see your identification and passport please?" the man at the passport control window asked.

The official looked at it, compared the photograph with the face before him, and wrote down the name: *Werner Hirn*. Also the number of the passport. Werner knew from his experience of last night that he would have to surrender his passport at this point and received in return a slip with a number on it. The passport went into a back room where no doubt it was inspected thoroughly and checked against any list of wanted criminals or those who might be listed as criminals because they had fled at one time from the German Democratic Republic. Once more Werner waited. As he stood there, he studied the faces of the others who were waiting in the long, barrackslike building. No one was relaxed. A tension common to each countenance was there. When his number was called, he went forward to a young lady in uniform who had his passport in her hand. She asked him how much money he had with him and he had to take it out of his wallet so that she could count it. On a pink form, she entered his 47 West German Deutschmarks. He knew he would have to exchange some of this at the next window at 1:1 even though the actual value was 1:3.

It took about an hour for Werner to complete his routine inside the building. When he went to his car, another Vopo officer came over and lifted up the hood to check the baggage section. He looked in the glove compartment, gave the package of fruit a cursory glance, and then spotted the package of cigarettes on the seat. Werner nodded and the officer skillfully slipped it into his pocket.

He was now free to enter the city of East Berlin. A sign

said, WELCOME TO BERLIN, THE CAPITAL OF THE GERMAN DEMOCRATIC REPUBLIC. It was a strange sensation for him to drive into the East Sector of the city. He had been here only a few other times in recent years since 1961 when the Wall had been erected. He remembered the despondent gloom of the place on those visits. He remembered the empty lots and the rubble. He remembered the desolate streets, the ghost-town atmosphere, the drabness of the buildings. This time it was different, somehow. Perhaps it was the sunshine of the August afternoon. Perhaps it was the lightness of his heart; after all, he was now free and unattached. And somewhere here in East Berlin there was the young lady he had met last night, the young lady with the lovely voice.

He had been with a group of students from Hamburg at the Cosmos Cafe on East Berlin's Karl Marx Allee last night. They had started out by themselves, but gradually they had begun to talk with some of the young people of their age from East Berlin. The conversation had begun easily enough with comments about music and sports. It had drifted to poetry and literature until it had come close to politics, and then both sides had suddenly started talking in riddles, Werner thought. He didn't want to talk politics, so he concentrated on a girl instead. He supposed she was from East Berlin, but that didn't matter. What mattered was that she had lovely hazel-green eyes that smiled when she looked at him and when she talked. He couldn't remember just what she looked like, but the eyes and the voice he could not forget. That voice, mellow and rich and resonant. He had never enjoyed listening to Gertrude's voice. But this girl with the green eyes had a cultivated Berlin accent that could have belonged to an actress. Maybe she was an actress, he thought. She had that sort of enviable aplomb. He really had not expected her to agree to meet him today, but it excited him to think that she had told him just where she would be in case he came.

14

He realized he had entered East Berlin farther south than the old place at the Brandenburg Gate which previously had brought him to Unter den Linden, so he turned up a cross street in order to get over to that familiar boulevard.

Driving down Unter den Linden, he looked for the landmarks that as a boy he had come to know so very well. On his left was the Memorial to the Unknown Soldier with two very Prussian-looking guards standing at absolute attention. On his right, the rebuilt State Opera House; and then, again on his left, the buildings of Humboldt University. If circumstances had been different, he might have attended this university, but because of the geography and politics of Germany during the first postwar years when he was at that age, he had attended instead the then-new Free University in West Berlin. The great Humboldt University, no longer the respected educational institution in Germany it had once been, now had a faculty where only the so-called "politically reliable" were allowed to teach.

Down past the Marienkirche on his right, he remembered having attended some organ concerts there with his parents when his father was still alive. Since his father was an organist himself, he tried to attend every special musical performance that time and budget would allow.

Nearby, the ruins of the great cathedral looked pathetic and forlorn in this citadel of materialism. He had been told they still held worship services in the undercroft. Across the street from the ruins was the Marx Engels Platz, a large square with a stadium-bleachers above on which a huge sign announced, THE DDR IS THE FUTURE OF GERMANY. Not a suggestion remained of the great palace that had once stood on that spot. It had been badly bombed during the war, and every stone had been removed.

Down near Alexander Platz at the center of the city he saw many new buildings under construction. For years East Berlin had remained static, in a kind of state of shock after the war, while West Berlin had built furiously. Now

15

it seemed clear that the regime in the East had decided to try their very best to catch up, and so they were building on all sides.

Because he was still very unfamiliar with the streets and particularly with the new street names in East Berlin, it took Werner longer than he thought to drive to the Ebenezer Church. His uncle was employed there as the custodian. He went around the building to a side door. He saw a bell and rang it. He waited. After a few moments the door opened and there was his uncle.

"Yes, yes, what would you like? What can I — oh, it's you, Werner!"

They shook hands and Uncle Klaus invited Werner into a little back room he had fixed up for himself near the vestry.

"Mother sent you this fruit and these cigarettes and I have a letter for you from her."

"And how is she? Happy to have her son home again, I'm sure."

"Yes, she smothers me with all the love in the world and I thrive on it."

He had to tell Uncle Klaus all about himself and his work of doing publicity for a film company in Hamburg. He suggested that his uncle open the letter and read it and, if possible, to write a little note in reply that Werner could take back to his mother. He knew how happy she would be to have the communication circuit completed.

While his uncle got out paper and pencil, Werner went out to have a look at the church. As he looked up at the altar and the pulpit, both filigreed with baroque angels and trumpets, and the old pews and the organ in the balcony at the rear, he was flooded with memories of his own childhood. He hadn't spent much time in churches in recent years, but there was a familiar feel to this place and a nostalgic kind of damp-stone-and-varnish smell to the old church building that reminded him of the many hours he had spent in churches as a boy. Many times he had sat and listened to his father play the organ at rehearsal and at church services and even at special concerts. Werner still considered himself a Christian, but he had successfully stored most thoughts of everyday religion on one of the shelves way back in his mind. None of his friends really took the church seriously either. Yet he knew he would resent having anyone label him as an unbeliever.

He wondered how he looked to these Berliners — to his mother and to Uncle Klaus. Did they see him as a successful young businessman, worldly-wise and sophisticated? Or was he still the uncertain fledgling student they had last known? Being in Berlin, particularly here in the East Sector where life was so radically different from his experiences in Hamburg, allowed Werner to see himself through new eyes. What he saw now, in bolder relief against these more primary concerns of life, rather disappointed him. His excitement-spangled life in a publicity agency for a film company suddenly came to have, from this remote vantage point, all the purposelessness of a ride on a garish, noisy carousel — gay, whirling activity without any real goal.

How did he look to those outside the orbit of his family and his religious and political group? He was eager to mix again and test his wits with the crowd he had met last night. That girl especially. He wanted very much to talk to her again. But before he could look for her, he had to give more of his time and attention to Uncle Klaus. His mother would expect that.

He returned to the little room in the back. "And you, Uncle Klaus? Tell me about yourself. How are things for you now over here?"

The old man smiled and then shook his head sadly. "These are difficult times. Yes, very difficult times. But I shouldn't bother you with that because you are young and are in the West and your life is full of hope and optimism and good fun, I think."

17

"But I'd like to hear about it. Where are you living now? In the same place?"

"Yes, but that is part of the trouble. I have a place over on Gutenbergstrasse. It's very near the . . . very near the Wall, you know."

"Then you saw it being built? You have a good view of it?"

"Yes, I'm afraid so. Things are very difficult for those who live near the Wall. It is necessary for us to have a special pass. No one can live there without it. All our activities are very closely watched. In that area the authorities are very suspicious. As you know, there have been many escapes attempted near our place. But I told the authorities I am just an old man, and only my housekeeper comes twice a week to clean. You know that after your aunt died I've been alone. I've been very lonely. And this nice old lady who lives here near the church agreed to come and clean my place and fix it up for me two times a week. Well, that was all right until three weeks ago."

"What happened then?" Werner asked.

"I don't like to talk about it and you shouldn't tell your mother. She would worry too much. But the functionaries actually suggested to me a most absurd thing — at least to me it was, and I wonder if they are at all civilized. Because my housekeeper does not live in our area, they did not want to give her a pass and that means I must fend for myself. Oh, I can get along but the arrangement was so pleasant the way we had it. When I spoke to the authorities about it they suggested that I marry the housekeeper! In this way they said I would be serving myself by having a full-time housekeeper and I would relieve the housing shortage by making her apartment available. That's Marxist logic for you!"

"Marry her? You're not serious?"

"I wondered, too, whether they were just playing a trick on me. I was ready to pass it off as a joke, but then they came back again and again and said the same thing to me.

18

Of course I won't marry her. It would be unthinkable! I do not love her and I could not think of a marriage of convenience. Imagine! At my age. It goes against everything I know. But they were serious about it. So what do I do? I just tell them: No! I must get along there alone or find a different place to live — if they'll let me. These are very difficult times, Werner. Especially for old people. The regime has no feeling for the Christian way . . . for the standards that we religious people hold dear. But you'd better not tell your mother all of this. She would worry too much."

Later, as Werner continued his drive down the streets of Berlin, the strange story that his uncle had told him would not leave his mind. The business of the Wall was bad enough, but the kind of callous lack of feeling of a suggestion like this to an old pious man who still lived with precious memories of his wife was to Werner a disgusting demonstration of Communist bureaucracy at its worst.

He had to stop and take out the map to find Mügelsee and the approach to the spot from which an excursion on the lake was to leave. She had said that she would be happy to see him again and if he wanted to join their party at the Mügelsee docks at two o'clock he might enjoy the trip. That was all he needed and he spontaneously had said that he'd meet her here.

He had hoped to see a milling crowd of people waiting to get on the boat. The place was empty now, but a big boat was at the dock. Perhaps they were all on board. Yes, he could see people on the boat. He went up to the ticket window and asked if he could still make the trip.

The man shook his head. "The boat leaves in ten minutes, but I'm sorry, it's all sold out."

"Are you sure? I'd planned so much on this trip. You see, I'm on my holidays and I had expected this to be the high light of my visit to East Berlin."

There was a pause as the man looked down at his list of passengers and then up at Werner. Then he said, "Well, you see, the excursion trips these days are pretty well filled up with groups from the factories, the collectives and all. They plan their outings long in advance and book for ten or twelve or twenty passengers, and there isn't much room left for those who come alone. But you are from West Germany, no?"

"Yes, I live in Hamburg."

"One moment, please. Let us at least try. You must not think badly of your brothers in East Berlin. After all, we should be good hosts to visitors from over there. Perhaps I can ask the captain. I won't promise, but at least I'll ask."

The man left his cage and hurried down the dock. He went aboard the boat to see what he could do. Werner studied the faces he saw on the deck to see if he could spot her. They were all busily talking and milling about, and he couldn't tell one from another. After a few minutes the man came back waving.

"The captain says we are all full but he says that one more won't really matter. So you can go aboard. The ticket is six marks."

As Werner sauntered through the crowd trying to spot his friend, he felt the other passengers examining him, although they were trying not to stare. He was aware that they were sizing him up and concluding that he was from the West. He figured that his clothes gave him away as he was better dressed than the average passenger.

Then he saw her! She was standing with a group of young men and women her age and she looked wonderful. Her hair was blowing in the breeze as she pointed to something on the opposite shore. Could he go up to her and announce his arrival? No. It would be better for him to ease his way over and let her notice him first.

He stood on the deck by the railing right next to a well-dressed elderly lady who was shepherding two young boys.

They wore the blue kerchiefs of the Young Pioneers. They were looking excitedly out to the water.

In between glances over to the main object of his interest, he studied the group to his left. The lady seemed to be the grandmother of the boys. From her clothes he guessed that she was from West Germany also and had come over to East Berlin to visit her family; perhaps she had wanted to do something special for the grandchildren and had invited them out on this excursion. From snatches of their conversation, he gathered that the youngsters were well on their way to becoming socialists. Werner knew that the Communist Party started its training program with the very young children in the Young Pioneers; later, as teen-agers, they were led into the Free German Youth; and finally, as adults, groomed for membership in the Communist Party itself. He caught such phrases as "The Farmer-Worker State" . . . . "The glories of socialism" . . . . "Peace and progress" . . . . "The warmongers of the West" — this from children who couldn't be more than ten or twelve years old!

Suddenly he felt a light tap on the shoulder. He turned quickly and there she was, smiling at him.

"I didn't think you'd come," she told him. "I thought you were only joking when you said you'd join us here today."

"Oh, I meant it all right. I'm a man of my word. And I've been looking forward to this. I'm glad I finally can have a chance to talk to you."

"Well, we'll have to try to give you a good time. Come and meet some of my friends." She indicated her group.

"But can't we talk — just the two of us?"

"Later. We'll have a chance to talk later. I mustn't be rude to the friends I came with. But how can I introduce you? I'm afraid I don't even know your name."

"That's been bothering me, too. I've been wondering what I should call you. I'm Werner Hirn."

"Well, I'm happy to meet you, Werner Hirn. And I'm Liselotte Lehman." She took him to her friends. After

21

she had introduced him to all of them and they had shaken hands, she said, "Herr Hirn is from the Federal Republic. He's come over to see the glories of Berlin. I hope we'll have a chance to prove to him that we're not such ugly people over here in the DDR, after all."

"On the contrary," he said quickly, "I think the scenery is delightful, both on the deck here and out on the water. Can I offer you something? How about over there at that refreshment stand? Maybe you'd like something to drink. May I?"

"Oh, no, Herr Hirn," said the tall fellow to his left. "After all, you are here in our country now. You are our guest." They all nodded and ushered him over to one of the tables near the lunch counter.

They were relaxed and somehow not relaxed, Werner felt. They were speaking in superficialities about the beautiful weather, about the beautiful lake, about all the people. Fräulein Lehman didn't talk very much and didn't seem really to be listening to the chatter of the others. Finally the short, sober-faced blonde girl next to Fräulein Lehman looked at Werner and said, "Tell us, Herr Hirn, are you active in politics in the Federal Republic?"

This was certainly a leading question. He thought it rather odd. It sounded so much like the kind of thing that would come only from a party member. He would have to be on his guard. It was to be expected, he supposed, that in a group like this there were all shades of political affiliation — those who were for the regime and those who, like most of the people in East Germany, were opposed to it and didn't discuss politics unless it was absolutely unavoidable. But the short blonde was expecting his answer.

"I'm afraid I'm much too busy to pay attention to political matters," he said. "Of course, I read the papers and I vote. I always feel I have a part in it when I am able to help select from among the various candidates."

22

"It is a pity that none of your candidates in the Federal Republic is really for peace, as we are."

He was thinking of what he might answer that would fit this particular barb when his Fräulein Lehman cut in and said, "Oh, let's not discuss politics today. We're on an outing. I think we should have a holiday from politics, too, don't you?"

The tall fellow raised his eyebrows and with a slight smirk spoke to her, "But, Comrade Lehman, everything in our society is political and we shouldn't miss an opportunity to correct some of the impressions that our friend from the West is likely to have about our country. After all, almost everything that is written in the warmongering press over there and on radio and television is distorted. Now that he is here, we should certainly give him the opportunity to ask any questions he may have."

"Oh, I don't think I have any questions. I'm here to enjoy myself." Werner smiled at everybody. Then he remembered those words he had heard: Comrade Lehman! Was the activist who said that only using his standard term because he assumed that everyone in his group was a comrade and a Party member, or was she really that? He would certainly have to find out. He wanted very much to talk to her alone; it seemed particularly difficult in this group.

Just then a seaplane zoomed over the ship and prepared to land on the lake. Everyone at their table jumped up and went over to the railing to watch the landing — all except Fräulein Lehman and Werner. For a few minutes at least they were alone.

"Now's our chance," he said. "Can't we go over to the other side and just talk, the two of us?"

"All right. I can see that you're not particularly enjoying this." She got up and they walked over to a safe distance from the others.

"And what shall we talk about?" she asked with a grin.

"Anything but politics. By the way, what's this about the 'Comrade' title he gave to you. Is it that?"

She looked away for a minute and then turned to him. She said in a purely emotionless voice, "Why of course. Didn't you see my pin? Only the honored members of the SED Party can wear this pin. I've been a member since I was twenty. And I gather that you're something else. Is that right?"

"Well, I'm not a member of any party, as a matter of fact. I'm certainly not a Communist."

Her eyes seemed to lose their sparkle as she looked into his. "Does it disappoint you that I am?" she asked him.

"Well, it surprises me, anyway. Somehow you didn't look like a Communist."

She laughed. "What did you expect? Horns and a tail? Really, you mustn't believe all the things that the press in the West says about us. We're really not so bad."

"At least I've discovered that a Party member can be charming and attractive. You see, I've never really had much of a chance to meet anyone like — well, like you. I'm afraid, though, that our ideals and principles and goals and standards are poles apart. I don't even know how to talk to a Communist."

"Well, maybe I can teach you. Lesson number one says: Communists are human beings. Lesson number two says: Communists are dedicated to the most noble achievements of science and technology and the salvation of the working class from their oppressors and are fighting the battle for peace. Does that sound so bad?"

"So here we are — talking politics. I guess over here you just can't get away from it, can you?"

"I promise you. Not one more word of politics for the rest of the trip. Agreed?"

She kept her promise. They walked and enjoyed watching the people and then joined the other group again. Werner said practically nothing. He had a sick feeling in his stomach — a kind of hunger. Initially he had been so attracted to this girl. She was so charming and lovely to be with that the last thing in the world he would have thought was that she could be a real-life Communist. Of course it couldn't go on. What could he possibly have in common with a person whose political and religious credo was diametrically opposed to his? He felt her sensing his disappointment; was this stimulating her to an extra effort to show him she could also be a woman?

When the ship came back to the dock and everybody prepared to disembark, he realized the time had come for him to say a final good-by. He might never see her again. Everything in his mind told him that he should shake hands with her, thank her for her courtesy, and forget the whole thing. Something else in the way she took his arm and smiled at him made him ask her instead, "Would you like a ride? I have a car and I'm driving back. I can take you home or any place you like."

"I'll see if I can gracefully escape from this group of comrades," she whispered to him. "I'd like to talk to you some more. You don't really know me yet."

"Good. That's my car over there. The green Volkswagen. Why don't you see if you can get away, and I'll wait for you."

She joined him, and as they drove along he had that strange heady sensation that comes from flirting with something dangerous. Forbidden fruit. But he had his eyes open, even though she was very attractive. So what possible danger could there be? He suggested that they stop to eat. She agreed. They drove up to a restaurant with a little terrace and garden with tables in the open air.

When they had ordered a snack and were sitting there, he said, "Now tell me about yourself. How did you ever get caught up in something so political?"

"I was raised on it. I inherited it. I never had a father whom I could remember, but I had a mother who was always a Party activist. She fed it to me from childhood. It was the most natural thing in the world that I, too, would go through the process and serve my country in the best way I knew how.

25

And you? Didn't you inherit your ideals and your views from your family, or did you somehow discover them quite by yourself?"

"Well, my parents tried," he said, "and I guess they succeeded, at least part way. My parents were very religious. My father was a church organist. I was raised in the church — the Evangelical Church, of course; I'm not a Catholic. My father died a few years ago and my mother feels that her Christian faith is the most important thing in the world to her."

"And you? Is your Christian faith important to you, too?"

"I guess I can only answer honestly. I won't pretend to be something I'm not. Yes, it's important for me to be a Christian; I mean I'd never give it up. But it isn't anything fanatical with me. As a matter of fact, it isn't something that I worry too much about. It's there when I need it."

"And does it help you when you need it?"

She was certainly zooming in on something that was embarrassing to him. It was true that he hadn't thought much about it, and here he was in the position of being interrogated about his religion, about his soul, by someone who was a practicing, believing Communist — which meant someone who was also a militant atheist.

"Well, let's just say I don't use it much. But that doesn't mean I've rejected it either," he added quickly. "It's too much a part of my tradition."

"We both have our traditions, I guess" she answered wistfully. "But more and more I believe that the things we believe and stand for have to be more than just traditions. After all, in Germany we have some pretty horrible traditions to live down. That is why it seems to me that the only hope is in our New Way. The world of the future will certainly not be based on superstitions and non-scientific ideas about God and heaven and angels and all that. These myths have brought us nothing but war and pain and grief and suffering."

He didn't quite know how to answer her. He knew he'd better get off the defensive and start on the offensive instead.

26

"And are you so sure that your way is right?" he asked. "It seems to me that there are plenty of indications that Communism has failed. It is every bit as much of a religion in the demands it makes upon its disciples as is Christianity."

"Well, I have to be honest with you, too, I guess, and say that I have some doubts. A good party member is supposed to confess his sins. They call it *self-criticism*. But we're never supposed to admit to somebody — somebody like you — that it's anything but perfection."

"As long as we've been so honest with each other, maybe our continuing to talk might get somewhere. You might even be converted away from Communism," he said, smiling.

"But I always thought one had to be converted to something better — not just away from something. As for me, everything that I've been taught to believe says that my duty is to convert you to Communism."

"It'll be quite a game, but I have only a short holiday — a month. So, when can I see you next?"

"I'm leaving for Leipzig tomorrow. My mother lives there. I have a job at the trade fair. I'll be gone for a week and a half."

"Well, then I guess I'll have to come to Leipzig," he replied half in jest.

"Why not? It's a wonderful place. I'd really be able to show you the 'glories of the new socialist order!' " She said it in a tone that admitted it was only a tired slogan she had been taught to parrot. "And as long as it's the Trade Fair, you might have some real business there, too. There are lots of visitors to the fair from all over the world. Why don't you try?"

"I might at that. How do I go about getting through?"

"No problem," she said with an air suggesting she could take care of everything. "But your business — you didn't tell me what you do."

"I'm a publicist . . . a kind of propagandist."

An ever-so-slight frown appeared on her face.

". . . for a film company," he added quickly.

27

"Well, then, perhaps you could be shopping for cameras. You have to have some commercial reason for going," she explained.

"Good. Give me your address and phone number in Leipzig and if I can make it, I'll look you up. And here's my address, in case you ever get over to West Berlin. What will you be doing in Leipzig?" He was looking for another piece of the puzzle.

She sighed and thought for a moment before answering. "I'm a publicist too. I'm on the news staff at Radio Berlin International. Sometimes I even get to read the news bulletins. You must tune in and listen for me. We're doing some broadcasts from the Leipzig Messe and I'm assigned to go along to help out. Try to come on Wednesday. Things will have settled down a bit by that time."

"Would it make any difference to you — really, now — whether I did come or not?"

Now her eyes met his with more genuine communication than at any time during their talk. The overtones in that look told him that there was a hidden meaning in what she answered: "I thought I was getting my point across. You still don't know me very well."

He decided at that moment that he wanted to know her better — much better, Communist or not.

2

WERNER PUT DOWN HIS CUP OF BREAKFAST COFFEE BY THE telephone. Immediately after he dialed the first three digits, he heard the metallic recorded voice on the line sputter, "Hamburg . . . Hamburg . . . Hamburg . . . Hamburg. . . ." It continued until he began dialing his office number. He asked to speak to his secretary. His mother overheard from the kitchen. She stopped her work to listen.

"Hello! This is Hirn. Yes, in Berlin. Please do me a special favor right away. On our letterhead, please send me a memorandum. Make it from Herr Wiehe and addressed to me. Here is what I want it to say:

> If it is possible for you, as we hope, to make appropriate travel arrangements to attend the Annual Fall Trade Fair in Leipzig, please investigate for our company the possibility of purchasing motion-picture-camera and sound-recording equipment in 35mm. If it is possible for you to run quality tests for us while you are there, this would be most helpful. Please report on your return.

As his mother came into the room where he was phoning, he noticed her but continued, "Do you have that? Yes, send it to me here in Berlin by air today — Express. You have the address. Good. And, Fräulein Zimmermann, please keep this confidential, understand? Good-by." He put down the receiver and met his mother's quizzical expression with a smile.

"Don't worry, dear. Just some business I have to take care of."

"But to Leipzig?"

"That's where the big fair is, Mother. It's safe to go. A lot of people from West Germany go."

"But, Werner, you're on vacation. I heard what you said on the phone. That was just a device, writing yourself a letter. I wasn't born yesterday. Don't forget I lived through the Nazi times. That's an old trick."

"There's nothing so sinister about it," he answered. "I'm interested in going to Leipzig and I need a commercial reason for going to the Messe. It's required. And I'll be glad to look at their cameras — if I have to."

She was still troubled. She felt awkward trying to talk to her son about her sudden anxieties. She didn't really understand him much any more. "Why this sudden interest in the east — the East Sector of Berlin — and the East Zone? Most people there look west and would love to get out, and they would come again by the thousands if the Wall weren't there. You know that, Werner," she said with a scolding tone in her voice.

He realized that he would have to reassure his mother. It was natural that she should worry and wonder why he wanted to go, and yet he didn't want to tell her there was a girl behind it all — a Communist girl. "That's exactly why I'm interested," he said. "I know very well what a prison it is in East Germany today. But while we still have the chance to get inside the country and look around, I think it is important to do just that."

She protested, "But it's not safe. They are always arresting this one and that one as spies. And don't forget, you were born there — in what is now the Zone."

"But I'm a West German. A resident of Hamburg. I have no police record or anything there to be afraid of," he argued.

She lifted her apron to wipe her face and her eyes. Then

30

she said, "You have no idea how dreadful it is for the people there now. Much worse than before. I know. Not only is my brother Klaus there, but my neighbor friend here, Mrs. Dreitlein, she has told me about her daughter in Freiberg. She gets some letters and reads between the lines. The lines themselves are bad enough. Mrs. Dreitlein's daughter was married to a doctor. There are three children. They stayed while others left because, as a doctor, he felt he belonged there to help the people as a doctor should. And the government wanted to keep him and so was fairly good to him. But then the poor man died. Now things are different for his widow. She must work and the children are being trained by the State. It is awful, I tell you."

"Of course it's awful. All the more reason to go in and see for myself," he said.

His mother didn't want to argue with him; he was too old for that. But still she didn't like it and hoped he might change his mind. Shrugging her shoulders, she went back to the kitchen. The name Leipzig started a train of thought for her that brought back many associations with people there and places she had visited with her husband. How he had loved Leipzig! It couldn't all have changed.

"Werner," she called out to him.

"Yes . . .?" He was getting on his coat, preparing to leave.

"If you do go to Leipzig, I wish you would . . . . Where are you going now?"

"I have to drive to the RIAS radio station to ask Fritz about getting a visa to the fair. What were you saying about Leipzig?"

Her eyes took on a less worried look. "I've been thinking about some of the places in Leipzig you must certainly visit, places your father loved to go. He'd like to think that you'd also appreciate them."

"Sure. I know. The Thomas Church."

She nodded. "Yes — try to hear a cantata there. They still give them regularly, you know. Bach is buried there, right in the church. And the great Bach museum. It is world famous. Did you know that your father once gave a recital on the organ in the Thomas Church? And Pastor Moser — I think he's still there."

It had been a long time since Werner had talked with Pastor Moser, who had confirmed him. His father had been the organist at the church where Pastor Moser preached. Whatever had happened to the spiritual reality of those days when he studied the catechism under the lively tutelage of Pastor Moser? He had made the Christian faith exciting. It was during the first few years after the war that Werner had discovered that man, Pastor Moser; since then he hadn't really been inspired by any man of God. He might have been, he thought, if he had followed the church line as his parents wanted him to — a career in church music or even the ministry.

Werner drove first to the RIAS building in the Schöneberg section to see Fritz Schumann. Fritz was part of the large staff of researchers of Radio-in-the-American-Sector, the station still operated by Americans for the purpose of sending the truth daily to the East Zone. It had been a spectacularly successful enterprise. Fritz and his colleagues monitored the DDR radio and pored over the local papers which they obtained from the various communities and cities to ferret out the important items because in the East Zone there was no national circulation of news. Rostock readers might never know what went on in Karl-Marx-Stadt, and even such a mundane thing as the rationing of butter or meat in one city would otherwise never be known in another.

As Werner drove up to the RIAS building and parked, he noticed what an interesting place it was with its curved front facing the intersection of four different streets. Like the Air Lift Memorial at Tempelhof, the Brandenburg Gate, and the charred ruins of the Kaiser Wilhelm Memorial Church, RIAS was a symbol to Berliners, a reminder of the unique role Berlin played in global politics.

He was glad that Fritz was so well informed on matters in East Germany. Fritz immediately telephoned to the East-West trade commission office and got the full particulars as to how Werner could get his application for a Messe visa and get it issued at a government bureau in East Berlin. If he wanted to drive his car he would also have to go through the process of applying for a special permit, and Werner did want to drive if at all possible.

When he returned, a visitor was waiting for him in the library at the house on Clayallee. His mother explained, "It's Mrs. Dreitlein, my neighbor. She has something to ask you. Please help her if you can."

Mrs. Dreitlein was a small, thin woman, with dark hair pulled back severely into a knot. Her lean face was taut with anxiety. Her hands were tightly clasped.

"You wanted to see me, Mrs. Dreitlein? What can I do for you?" he asked.

She hesitated, not knowing how to begin. "Your mother mentioned you were planning to go to the Zone."

Werner looked at his mother, expressing some surprise that she had mentioned this, but she was only nodding encouragement to Mrs. Dreitlein.

"Yes, I'm planning to go, if I can get a permit."

"Well, it would be the answer to my prayers if you could take a message to my daughter in Freiberg."

"Is that on the way to Leipzig?" Werner asked.

"No, not really. It's a little south and west of there. But perhaps you could drive that way, either coming or going. Do you think so?" she pleaded as she asked it.

Werner remembered the limitations Fritz had described to him. "It's not likely, I'm afraid, Mrs. Dreitlein. I understand we West Germans can travel only on the Autobahn from Berlin to Leipzig and can't leave it to make any side trips. I'm sorry. Otherwise I would be glad to take the message." He saw the disappointment in her face. "Is there any other way?"

"But perhaps you could ask," she said. "Maybe they would give you special permission or something."

"Perhaps I could telephone your daughter from Leipzig," Werner suggested.

"Too dangerous, I fear. This is a very important and secret message."

"Secret?"

Mrs. Dreitlein looked at Werner's mother for some cue. She got it with a quick nod and said, "You see, I must get my daughter and her children out of there. It's unbearable for them. I know it. And the message is about my plans for that."

"You have plans?"

Again Mrs. Dreitlein hesitated. The muscles of her cheeks twitched. She said, "Yes, partly. But we need to establish a code so that when I am ready to have her come to East Berlin, I can send a special telegram and she will know what it means."

The Wall did not completely stop the human flow from East to West of those who wanted to escape. Werner knew very well that there were spectacular attempts made from time to time to jump over the Wall or crash through it or tunnel under it. Some refugees had been killed in the attempt; the Vopos on border duty had orders to shoot to kill any persons fleeing.

"There aren't many ways across any more that haven't been discovered. It could be very dangerous. Are you sure you're not just making it worse for them?" he asked.

"I've thought about that, of course. But if some can still do it, why not my daughter and my grandchildren? It's like the Nazi times, or worse. At that time we told ourselves, 'It is bad, but it will soon get better. If we do nothing, it will all pass!' Well, by now we have learned that some did have the spirit to resist and others lived to regret their lack of courage. The question is, Is it worth it? I have answered it. It *is* worth the chance."

34

Werner's mother spoke up. "Perhaps you could have some business in Freiberg, Werner."

"What do you mean? What kind of business?"

"Like your business in Leipzig. You know. Something that would be believed, like your camera business, to serve as an excuse."

Werner opened his hands in an I-don't-know-what-it-would-be gesture. "What do they have in Freiberg?"

Mrs. Dreitlein brightened. "They have the uranium mines there. These were very important to the Russians and maybe they still are."

"That would be too risky. I couldn't dream up anything connected with uranium, of all things."

"The school of mines? There is a well-known school of mines there."

He shook his head.

His mother had an idea. "The cathedral! A great church. One of the best Silbermann organs in the world, I think. Couldn't you ask to see it and hear it?"

"Why? What reason could I give?" he asked. They sat silent for a moment. "I suppose I could invent something, like wanting to use it in a film production. Of course, I don't have anything to do with production, but my company could be interested. Perhaps I could ask to have it recorded. I could get a letter from my office." He winked at his mother and she smiled her assent.

"Well, I can't make any promises, Mrs. Dreitlein, you know that. But I'm willing at least to try."

3

Frau Lehman's apartment had all the comforts of home
that three small rooms and a kitchen and bath would allow
in busy crowded Leipzig. And yet the apartment didn't
seem like home to her daughter. Lise felt like a visitor,
almost like an intruder.

Strange, she thought, how she still had a secret yearning
for really belonging to her mother, if not to her mother's
world. It had been strongest when she was a child. Oh,
there had been wonderful times when Lise and her mother
had seemed like normal natural people — like a real mother
and daughter. Lise had retained in her memory vivid
details of the holidays when just the two of them would
tramp through the woods and swim in the lake and go to
concerts and read together in some of the classics. These
had been rare, isolated times. Mostly, when her mother
was working — and she worked very hard at a variety of
organizational jobs for the Party — Lise had felt like some
necessary branch, appropriately labeled, on one of her
mother's organization charts.

Today Frau Lehman was making phone calls again —
arrangements with a succession of people — some she called
Genosse or Comrade, others simply Herr Braun or Fräulein
Schmitt or Frau Wolf. Listening for a while, Lise soon got
tired of that and puttered around in the kitchen. Her mother
was a dreadful housekeeper. Her penchant for organization

and detail certainly did not extend to her own living quarters. It had always been like this. Whenever Lise came to visit — this had been less and less frequently in the last years since she had been in Berlin — she spent half of her time putting her mother's house in order. There were scraps of old food to be disposed of, and cups and wine bottles and greasy dishes that had stood for days on the shelf. Lise herself was naturally neat and liked to have things clean and tidy.

She wondered why she was different in this respect, and in a number of other ways, too. Maybe this was her way of reacting against the authority and dominance of her mother. Or maybe it was the result of her years and years and years in the state schools that became, intentionally, a disciplinary substitute for the home. Discipline! She had had her fill of it. Especially in the Party's school where she was drilled in the dialectic of Marxism and Leninism until it became so automatic that she could react like one of Pavlov's dogs to a bell and when the right cue came she would find herself giving voice to the proper words and phrases.

She had found no real satisfaction in the training in which she had been immersed so long. The problem of saturation was not recognized by the Party's educational functionaries; they pressed for supersaturation. There was constant and never-ending repetition to a point of almost hypnotic acceptance. If a phrase or a point of logic was repeated often enough it would become a part of you. The luxury of freely examining an opposing viewpoint, or even an opposing fact, was not permitted.

Lise returned to the cluttered combination library-sitting-work room. From the phone her mother looked up and smiled at her. Lise smiled back. It was a little thing and purely automatic but the moment was a satisfying one even so. The words exchanged between them — and there had been few so far on this visit — were only rarely real and meaningful.

Where to start on this mess? Papers and pamphlets and books . . . clippings and photographs and Messe literature all over. Her mother finally finished her call.

"Well, Lise, here we are. Just like old times, isn't it? Tell me about Berlin."

Frau Lehman was a woman of fifty-two. Her figure had become plump and saggy. Her hair was short and frizzy and speckled with gray. She lit a cigarette and offered one to her daughter who gestured a refusal. She puffed heavily and leaned back to stretch. Comrade Brigitte Lehman relaxed only for a minute. Then she collected herself and tuned up her muscles again as if she would be ready at a moment's warning to reach for the phone or to pound something out on the typewriter.

"I like Berlin, Briggi," Lise started. She always called her mother that now. She remembered when it had started because her mother was once embarrassed when a functionary had told her — Lise was eighteen then — that she didn't look old enough to have a grown daughter. "I have a small room and a little kitchen. It's adequate. In Ober Schöneweide. I can walk to the radio station."

"Where are your Party meetings? At the studios?"

"No, only sometimes. Mostly the group meets at the SED sports arena nearby on Grünauer Street. But I don't go very often."

Her mother reacted exactly as she knew she would. Her face was set in disappointment. Her eyes focused sharply on Lise as she asked, "And why not?"

"Well, in the first place, we're busy day and night, and, in the second place, the meetings are a bore. Really. No one at the station takes them seriously. We don't go unless it's made clear that we have to."

"What kind of discipline do they have in Berlin anyway? I've heard there is more laxity there than here. They let things go on right under their noses that they would not tolerate down here."

38

Lise laughed. "But this is the Worthy Goat's own Saxony!"

"Liselotte Lehman! I don't appreciate your speaking of Comrade Ulbricht in that manner."

"Oh, Briggi, don't be such a prude. You know everyone calls him that. You should hear some of the Berlin comrades when they get a little too much to drink at a party. Then you can tell what they really think!"

"I would have hoped you would have remained more correct in your Party responsibilities, Lise. You'll suffer for it sometime, if you don't. Take it from me — I know the Party backwards and forwards — there is no room, really, for deviationism."

"Briggi, please! I listen to that line fifteen hours a day. I even feed it out over the air like an obedient disciple of the Party. Can't I even let down my hair in my own . . . in the home of my own mother?"

Her mother lit another cigarette. "I'm worried about you. You seem so cynical. Please don't disappoint me — I've dreamed that you might go even higher in the Party than I have gone. You have such a perfect opportunity in Berlin. I have been so proud of you — sometimes I have listened when you broadcast! Imagine, my own daughter as the voice of the DDR to the whole land! It must give you a thrill."

"It's work. And often very boring and dull work."

"I don't understand. I don't understand at all. Isn't there a sense of being in touch with thousands and millions of our citizens — to say nothing of those on the other side?"

Lise was getting disgusted. Did she have to treat her mother like every other functionary and tell her exactly what she wanted to hear? Or could she speak candidly and bluntly?

"Who are we fooling except ourselves?" Lise said. Yes, she was cynical and didn't really care. "Who listens to our Radio Berlin International . . . our voice of the people of the great German Democratic Republic? I'll tell you. Not

39

the people. They listen to RIAS and watch TV from the West. You know it, I know it, everyone knows it. But we pretend it isn't so. Why, even the faithful Party members listen and watch Western programs when they dare. Even the functionaries. Of course I can listen officially right in my office."

"You actually listen to RIAS?"

"Certainly! How else would we know what there is to deny on our own broadcasts? RIAS says something . . . we check with the information section. If it's dangerous, we deny it and attack the 'gutter station that wants to bring the counter-revolution to the DDR.' Oh, I know the line: 'Behind RIAS and other such organizations are the hidden machine guns of the militarists. They peddle a poison that can have terrible consequences.' And so on, and so on, and so on."

Her mother snapped back, "But it's true. They do peddle poison."

Lise sighed, "Sure, sure. The Party says so, so we must believe it. I believe it on one side of my mind and on the other side I remember what I hear on RIAS. *You* don't listen to it so you have no choice but to accept the Party's interpretation."

"There is no other correct interpretation. I always accept the Party's judgment."

"Always?"

"Of course. Don't you?"

"You taught me I should," Lise answered, "and I would like to. But I can't believe that something is black and white at the same time. We warn against the revanchist militarism of the Federal Republic, and then we turn around and order complete military conscription of young men here. We cite case after case of militarism in the West, and then our soldiers, not theirs, learn to goose-step, like their fathers under the Nazis."

Her mother began to protest. Lise held up her hand and said, "Don't bother to give me the answers explaining these

40

contradictions. I am an expert at rationalizing on the Party line. I do it every day. And I'll keep on doing it. But do we have to keep on pretending that it's right or that it makes sense?"

Then her mother spoke. "Whatever serves the Party is right and makes sense, and don't forget it." Her tone was scolding and angry.

"I'm sorry, Briggi," Lise said with the proper note of penitence in her voice. "I just needed to blow off steam, I guess. I've been working hard. And I'm home now and I thought at least here I could get it out of my system."

Her mother looked down at the floor for a moment. "I'll try to forget this. But for your own good, keep your eyes straight ahead on the goal of our Party — don't be tempted by the lies you hear from RIAS or anywhere else."

And wear blinders like a work horse, Lise thought to herself.

The phone rang. "Lehman," her mother said crisply into the phone. A pause. "Oh, . . . Yes, she is here. A moment, please." She handed the phone over to her daughter.

It was Werner. She'd have to be careful. "Good afternoon, Herr Hirn. Welcome to Leipzig. What can I do for you?"

"When can I see you?" he asked.

"Oh, yes, the exhibit. Of course. Well, I'm very busy with my radio assignments, but perhaps I could. What is your schedule?"

He played along. He assumed that the first voice he had heard was her mother. "My schedule is . . . is flexible. You name it and I'll be there. Just give me the place and time."

"I am very sorry, Herr Hirn, I'm afraid I can't."

"Can't? Can't what?" he asked. Then he realized he had to feed her the right questions. "Oh, you mean you can't name the time and place? But you do want to see me, don't you?"

"That's right, Herr Hirn."

"Good. Well, I'm at the Foreign Visitors Section now.

How about here in an hour?" He waited for her response.

"Why don't you go to the Press Center, Herr Hirn, say about five o'clock. Do you know where that is? Just down Schillerstrasse from where you are now to the corner of Petersstrasse. Is that all right?"

"Fine. I'm staying at the International Hotel."

Lise saw her mother making some notes. "Well, I'll try to make it. But if something unforeseen comes up, I'm sure any of the young ladies at the Press Center will be able to help you. Thank you for calling. I hope you enjoy your visit in Leipzig."

Her mother didn't wait for an explanation. "Who is this Herr Hirn you're meeting?"

"A young man I met in Berlin. When I heard him say he was coming to Leipzig I suggested that he call me in case I could be of help to him. I told him about the exhibit and the Press Center and I'll show it to him," she answered.

"There are guides for that sort of thing."

Lise didn't want to have to discuss the matter, but her mother detected something not quite normal about it. "I wanted to help him myself, that's all."

"Where's he from? What's his first name."

"Werner Hirn. He's from Hamburg."

Frau Lehman lit another cigarette. "Hamburg! You'd better be mighty careful, Lise. The Federal Republic probably sent him here as a spy."

"Briggi, how ridiculous! He's just a businessman."

"All spies from there are just businessmen. It's common knowledge. How did you happen to meet him in Berlin?"

Lise felt awkward under her mother's insistent probing. "You really have to know everything, don't you?"

"Is there any reason I shouldn't?"

"I just met him casually. He was with some of my friends. I've been taught to use every opportunity to convince our friends from the Federal Republic of the glories of our socialist state. A little honey catches a lot of flies.

42

I know all about it. This is my job on the radio, remember?"

Her mother seemed ready to dismiss it. "You'd better be right," she said. "By the way," Frau Lehman added, "don't plan anything for tonight. I'm taking you along to a party. It's at the Press Center — eight-thirty."

Lise smiled but inwardly winced. "How nice. I hope I don't have to work."

"There'll be some very important comrades there. I want you to become known by the right people. It's quite an honor for me to be invited and to be able to take you along."

Lise decided to go out for a walk. She was badly in need of some fresh air.

4

WERNER STOOD IN THE PHONE BOOTH, HOLDING THE PHONE IN his hand for a moment. Was he crazy to have come all the way to Leipzig just because of a girl? And what a girl he had picked! A real Red, a Party-liner, an admitted Communist. Was he that naïve — didn't he know enough about what the Communists had done in East Germany to reject the idea? But he had told himself again and again that he had his eyes wide open. It was a flirtation with danger that appealed to him and gave him a kind of thrill.

But what could it come to? The East Germans, including Lise, and specifically Lise because she was part of the system, were held here in their zone behind barbed wire and a wall. One huge concentration camp! What could it come to with him and her? Could he fall in love with her? She was fun to be with, he knew that. She was physically attractive and he had to admit a magnetic pull from her sex appeal. But love is more than an emotional fling with a beautiful woman. Gertrude was pretty, too. Really lovely. He still thought so. He had been more intimate with her than with any other girl he'd ever dated, but she had principles, and wouldn't let him go too far. What would it come to with Lise? Did she have principles, too? What did Marx and Lenin have to say about this? As yet he'd hardly touched her, and now here he was in Leipzig pursuing her.

He left the phone booth and went to fill out the forms in the large hall where uniformed attendants sat behind tables, each with a sign for a different language offered: Russian, Spanish, Chinese, Polish, Yugoslav, and English. The first step was to register with the police. This wasn't just the simple little form that every European hotel has, but a form with questions as to the time of arrival, expected departure, business at the Messe, plus the usual passport information and hotel location while in Leipzig. Werner didn't have a reservation so he had to go over to the accommodations desk and request a room. There was no problem; he was booked into the International Hotel, which catered to Fair visitors from abroad.

Werner wasn't really prepared for the way in which he was treated as a foreigner. He was a German and this was Germany, too; and although there was an obvious political difference, they were the same people. But he got the cold treatment. Nothing rude was said; it was all very correct and formal. But there was no feeling of his being among his own German people. It gave his whole trip an overtone of tension. He was self-conscious here of everything he said or did. He couldn't escape the feeling that he was being sized up and down by everyone. Maybe it just seemed this way to him because all of the workers and officials in this reception area wore Party pins and were obviously Party regulars. He almost laughed out loud when he remembered that he had come here in order to be with just such a person.

He had until five to meet Lise. He had better get squared away at his hotel and apply for his permit to visit Freiberg on the return trip.

He found the visa office on Katherinestrasse within walking distance from the International Hotel. He explained to the receptionist what he wanted and she referred him to a department on the second floor. A Vopo there handed Werner a long form to fill out.

After waiting in line for about twenty minutes, Werner was ushered into the office of the director of the police visa bureau. He motioned Werner to sit down and asked for his passport, Messe visa, and application. He looked over the papers and then left to talk with someone in the next room, taking the documents with him. Through the closed door, Werner could hear them, but the words weren't distinct enough to be understood. *They're checking me out,* Werner concluded, *and giving my passport the usual security examination for forgery and looking to see if my name is on any special lists. We'll see now if I pass the test.* The officer returned. "Why Freiberg, Herr Hirn?" he asked.

Werner told him again what he had written, that the Freiberg organ was outstanding and that he would like to have it tested for possible use for a motion-picture sound track.

"I'm afraid that all matters pertaining to films and filming have to be handled by DEFA. You know DEFA, of course, our state film production agency?" the police official asked in a neutral tone, neither warm nor cold.

"And can I see DEFA here in Leipzig and get this arranged?"

"Possibly," answered the man. "However, as you know, the usual procedure is to clear this with DEFA at their headquarters in Berlin; but you might check at the Messe office and see whether you can speak to their people here. Yes, that would be best." The man handed the documents to Werner. He was dismissed.

On his way back to the hotel, Werner looked in the shop windows and noticed a small philatelist shop with a special display of Messe stamps in the window. He stopped to buy a postal card and a commemorative stamp. Then he wrote to his mother that it didn't seem possible to hear the great Silbermann organ after all. She would know what that meant and could tell her neighbor, Mrs. Dreitlein.

Ambling on, he came to the big Rathaus square where

46

the old famous Leipzig City Hall stood, a glorious building with its colorful roof and walls — a vignette from the Middle Ages. The many-tiered walls and spires with their ginger-bread figurations reminded him of Hamburg's Rathaus, and the other Hanseatic cities. Beyond the square, he reached Thomasgasse. He knew this would lead to Thomas Church which his mother wanted him to visit. Perhaps there would be time later.

His hotel had no atmosphere of cordiality. Its lobby was drab and austere. The building, though functional and adequate, had no style. He was about the only one there who was alone. Little groups of visitors walked by, chatting in a variety of languages. A huge portrait of bearded Comrade Ulbricht dominated the lobby.

In his room Werner took off his shoes and lay down on the bed. He had almost three hours until his rendezvous with Lise. Would there be time to visit Pastor Moser? He decided to take a taxi to Pastor Moser's home rather than to drive his own car in a strange city. So that he wouldn't call attention to his visit by arriving conspicuously at Pastor Moser's house, he asked the taxi driver to stop a block away. Werner knew that there were informers in every block in the East German cities. No need to bring any suspicion on the old pastor, who probably had difficulties enough.

He rang the bell and waited a full minute without any response. Then he rang again. The door was opened by an elderly lady.

"Is Pastor Moser at home?" he asked.

She hesitated. "A moment please, I will see."

"Tell him that Werner Hirn is here." She disappeared and returned in a few minutes.

"Please come in." Werner followed her inside and up two flights of stairs. The old lady knocked on the door. Presently it was opened and a short, heavy man stood there. He looked at Werner a few seconds, and then a broad smile broke out on his round face.

47

"Werner, my boy! Werner Hirn! What a perfectly wonderful surprise! Come in, come in. Let me look at you."

The sight of Pastor Moser overwhelmed Werner. He had begun to feel like an outcast in Leipzig, like an unwanted stranger. But here, immediately, he was enveloped with a secure feeling of belonging — like a flashback to the old family circle with his father and mother and cousins and aunts and uncles where he had been a part of the traditions and *Gemütlichkeit* of warmth and love and friendship.

The study was a familiar place to Werner, even though this was a different house, a different room. He recognized the books, the busy work desk filled with papers, and the lingering aroma of a pipe. Pastor Moser excused himself from the room. Werner looked around. He examined the book titles on the well-filled shelves. There were mostly theological books, but in one section he saw an interesting collection of novels in English and French and German.

There were a number of pictures on the wall — groups of people from various congregations he had served. Werner's heart quickened as he saw a picture of his father with Pastor Moser. He looked at it a long time and only turned away when his host returned to the room.

"I was going to show you that." Pastor Moser came up and put his arm around Werner and looked at the picture with him. "Your father was a splendid man, Werner, a real Christian man, and a dear friend of mine. I miss him, and hundreds of his old friends miss him, too. Now, sit down, please, and tell me all about yourself. What brings you to Leipzig?"

"The Fair," Werner answered. What should he tell him about the purpose of the trip? "Actually, I'm on my vacation. I've been spending a little time in Berlin with my mother, and I had the chance to see something of Leipzig and East Germany by coming to the Messe."

"And how is your mother?" the pastor asked.

"She's doing well, thank you. She is the housekeeper for

a Berlin family. They are gone for the summer, so I can stay there a month with her. I'm enjoying it."

"And what about you? What is your work? Where do you live?"

As Werner told him about his publicity duties for a film company in Hamburg, Pastor Moser leaned forward with genuine eagerness to hear the details of his assignments and how he accomplished them.

"I'm afraid we don't get those same films over here. The pictures made on this side are very bad and the Russian films are worse."

"But tell me about how it is for you, Pastor," Werner said. Pastor Moser nodded and then, before he spoke, he carefully put a teapot warmer over the telephone.

"Well, we remain happy and we work very hard and God is good to us, so we must be thankful." The pastor paused and then looked seriously for a moment into Werner's eyes. His face became somber. "But these are difficult times. Very difficult times. Perhaps you know how it is."

Werner explained that he was aware of the fact that the churches were under considerable pressure by the regime, and he supposed it was probably worse since August Thirteenth and the Wall, "But I'd like to know from you how it *really* is," he added.

"The Church in the DDR is allowed to exist. There is no persecution in the sense that they forbid us to preach or to have worship services. Rather, it is a subtle thing, a psychological harassment that shows up in so many ways. But the number-one problem is the youth. This is where our main battle is fought. You know about the Youth Pledge?"

"Yes, isn't it a kind of substitute for confirmation?"

Pastor Moser got up and went to draw a picture folio out of his book shelf. He turned some pages. "Here. Do you recognize this?"

It was a class of over one hundred boys and girls on the front steps of a large church. Werner knew it at once. It was St. Michael's Church where his father had been the church musician right after the war. Werner scanned the group and found himself. "Why, of course! I remember it very well. How nice that you keep this."

"But look at my last year's class — here." Pastor Moser flipped the pages to the back of the book.

There were seven young persons, four girls and three boys. "So small?" Werner asked.

"That's the difference. It's not that there are fewer teen-age youngsters today. On the contrary, there are more now, of course. But the State has made it almost impossible for the young people to avoid being 'confirmed' in the Communist ritual of *Jugendweihe*. And we don't accept the idea that one can promise his life and devotion to materialism one day and to God the next. Instead, we have moved confirmation up two years to make sure that those who make their promise to follow the Lord Christ really mean it."

"So you're really losing the battle for the youth?" Werner said.

"In numbers, I guess you would have to say so," the pastor agreed. "But one result of this — and the other competitions the State places against us — is that active Christians are taking the whole idea of confirmation and the sacraments much more seriously today. Now in the DDR people don't just go to church from habit or because it's the right thing to do, to make a good showing in the community. In this society, going to church is the *wrong* thing to do. A young person may have to pay for it in many ways. Those who come to communion come because they really want it and need it and attendance has increased since the Wall. This is not all bad. It's something like a refining fire."

The way this man talked so calmly about the life-and-death struggle of his church deeply impressed Werner. But as his pastor continued, Werner felt also a growing embarrassment at what he knew was his own defection from the confirmation pledge he once made to God. It almost seemed as if Pastor Moser sensed this as he continued to talk, although there was no suggestion that he knew the secrets of Werner's own heart.

"Look at it this way. Let's suppose your class back then — it was '47 wasn't it? — were faced with some of the same choices they have today. What would have happened? Oh, I remember there were other problems then right after the war — what to wear, what to eat, how to get over the shock of the destruction of our land. But you now in West Germany with your prosperity, you never think of that any more. Here, too, for the most part, we forget, except we still have rationing of food — butter, meat, and now and then even potatoes.

"What would have happened in your confirmation class if you had been hungry — you remember, Werner, what it was like to be really hungry? — and then if you had gone to church on Sunday and if you had chosen confirmation instead of *Jugendweihe*, your parents would have had difficulty getting ration coupons. The authorities wouldn't have said 'No, you can't have them,' but they would have delayed and complicated it and you would still not have been able to buy the food. You would have had poor marks in school because your church activity would have been evidence that you were not 'politically reliable.' And then, just at the time that your catechism class was to have met or at the time when you were supposed to have sung in the choir, the school or the Young Pioneers or the Free German Youth would have made it compulsory for you to attend a special meeting or a rally or to join a work brigade. If under those circumstances you had had to choose, which would you have chosen?"

Werner really wondered. The question could not be answered from his viewpoint now. But back then, he had been young and idealistic and inspired by both his parents and Pastor Moser, and he believed he might have been en-

51

couraged by them to choose the Christian way. How could he really know?

"I don't know what I would have done," answered Werner. "I guess if my record in recent years is any indication, I would have taken the easy way out." There — he had spoken honestly. He half expected the pastor to shake his finger at him, he was that self-conscious in the presence of this tower of spiritual strength.

"I ask myself what I would have done, too," said Pastor Moser. "We never know. We can only pray that when these questions come we will do the right thing."

"How many really make the hard choice?" Werner asked.

"You mean here in my parish or in all of the DDR? But it's about the same. Ninty-five percent of the people compromise their beliefs and do what the State tells them to do in most things where they would have to pay a price by doing otherwise. I think it fair to say that only five percent of the people decide they must stand fast and choose on the basis of their Christian faith when the issue is drawn."

"Five percent?" Werner thought this sounded like an alarmingly low figure.

But before he could consider just what it meant the pastor said, "I wonder if it would be any different in the West. What do you think?"

This didn't reach him at first. "You mean if we had those same problems?"

"No, I mean now . . . with the choices you have to make every day in your prosperous, carefree society. Isn't it the same there also — a choice between the worship of man and the worship of God? But how do your people choose? Are your churches full every Sunday? Do fifty percent go . . . or thirty . . . or perhaps ten?"

Werner could not quite look into the eyes of his host. "I'm afraid I don't know the answer to that."

"Forgive my lecture. I can't change from the role of

52

pastor. And I still like to think I am your pastor, too. But perhaps you can see why I say that under the pressures we have from an anti-religious regime, we are building something stronger, at least among those few who remain faithful. History has shown that when the Church has to fight for its life —"

The study door opened and a gray-haired woman entered. The men stood up. She came towards Werner smiling and held out her hand. It took a moment for him to recognize Frau Pastor Moser.

"Welcome to Leipzig" she said. It's been almost ten years . . . no, more than that . . . since I've seen you. You have become such a handsome young man."

"It's wonderful seeing you again. My mother asked me to bring you her greetings," Werner responded.

Frau Pastor announced that tea was ready in the next room. They all went in and sat down at a table where there was a plate of open sandwiches, some cookies, and some pastry. They chatted about old times, about Werner's father and his years of faithful service and his beautiful organ playing and choir directing. Frau Moser remembered little things about Frau Hirn and inquired about all the other Hirn children and where they were now.

"Werner is a businessman now in Hamburg," the pastor said to his wife. "He's come to visit the Messe."

"Oh, did your company send you?" she inquired.

"No, not exactly, but I have that as the official excuse for being here." He wasn't ready to share with them the real reason. As Werner thought about it, he wondered what these good Christian folks would think if he said he came here to meet a girl from East Berlin that he had seen twice in his life — a lovely young Communist girl. The thought of his apparent hypocrisy gnawed at him. But at least he hadn't pretended to Pastor Moser that he was still a practicing churchgoer.

Later, as he walked to find a taxi, he tried to have a

dialogue with his conscience. Pastor Moser's final words at the door haunted him: "Let me repeat the words I spoke to you at your confirmation when I shook your hand at the altar and gave you the Bible verse that was to be your own *Spruch* to carry with you always. You remember it, I think. Carry it with you now, also: 'Fight the good fight of faith.'"

As he walked along, Werner thought about this. His visit to this good man and his wife took him back to another time. He was young then and easily swayed by the dynamic personality of his pastor. He felt this same strong force again today. But sixteen years is a long time. His interests had taken on new and different and more exciting dimensions. He was enmeshed in the stimulating life of a film publicist. What did the "good fight of faith" have to offer him now? Was he so naïve that a little nostalgic excursion back to an emotional crisis of his youth would change him now when he was thirty years old? He still had the faith, after all. Yes, but he wasn't fighting for it.

He saw a taxi. It would get him to the Press Center to meet Lise at five.

The Press Center was closed. There was a man at the reception desk who said all the exhibits had been shut down until tomorrow because of a special party this evening. Werner decided to wait at the main door for Lise. He read the propaganda signs in the lobby and read them again as he waited. He stepped outside to wait for a while. No Lise. After forty-five minutes, he concluded that she wasn't coming. Puzzled, he went back to his hotel.

The lobby of the International Hotel was jammed with Fair guests. While he waited in line at the reception desk for his key, he picked up a folder with a map of the city listing the restaurants and entertainment spots recommended to the Fair visitors.

As he opened the door of his room and went in, he immediately sensed that someone was there. He closed the door and saw her behind it. Before he could recover from

54

his surprise and call her name and ask her what this was all about, Lise put her finger to her lips for silence. She pointed to the chandelier. He didn't immediately understand. Then she pointed to her ear and again at the light fixture. Of course! The room might be wired with a hidden microphone . . . or maybe she knew it really was.

She led him over to the desk, took a pad of paper and her pen and wrote hastily: *Sorry I couldn't come to the Press Center. I'll explain later. Can you meet me in the park?* He nodded his agreement. She looked at her watch. *Twenty minutes from now?*

He took the pen and wrote: *Where? What place?*

She wrote out her answer: *Across Richard Wagner Strasse.* Then she took the folder he had in his hand and opened it to the map of the city. She marked a place in the corner of the park, just two blocks from the hotel. She started to leave and then returned and took the pad of paper again.

You may be followed, she wrote, *so take evasive action and lose any escort.*

He nodded his head to assure her he understood. Then she took the two sheets on which they had written, put them in the ash tray and lit a match to them. They watched them burn. She took the ashes into the bathroom and flushed them down the toilet. Then she put on her gloves and went to the door. She turned and smiled at him.

Werner went towards her. This was a crazy moment in this weird, mysterious game of silence. But her coming like this to his room said more to him than a book full of words. He had something he wanted very much to "say" to her and any words he might use would be inadequate anyway. She looked poised and unperturbed, but he sensed from her eyes and her stance that she was full of tension. He came close to her and gently touched her arm. She stiffened and looked at him with a strange question in her eyes. Then he put his arms around her and held her close until she relaxed. He tenderly touched his lips to hers.

She closed her eyes, and her arms found their way around him as she offered her lips again in a hungry kiss. He saw that her eyes were filled with tears. She shook her head, turned to open the door, and quietly went out.

For a few seconds he couldn't move. The emotional recall of the scene sent a tremor through his body and he felt as though he had downed some instantly intoxicating elixir. He delayed facing the meaning of this mysterious rendezvous, and holding the sensation aloft, he walked slowly to the wash basin and splashed his face with cold water.

Then he realized he was afraid; not of her, although reason would say he really should be, but mostly afraid of the strange and bizarre situation that he couldn't have anticipated. And Werner was afraid also of himself. Where would this lead? What would come next? Should he escape now before any more strands of the web entangled him? He couldn't, of course. He had to follow through and find out what had prompted her to do what she did.

He went out and took the elevator, not to the ground floor but to the second floor. He found the stairs and went down to the lobby. He tried to appear nonchalant. Was anyone waiting for him at the elevators? He had his key in his hand but slipped it into his pocket, large and awkward though it was, to avoid identifying himself at the reception desk. He walked out and went to the corner. He waited for the traffic light. He looked back at the hotel. People were coming toward him but no one left the hotel and came in his direction when he stood there. He crossed Richard Wagner Strasse to the park. He checked his map to get his bearings and walked much more slowly than he wanted to. When he found her, she was sitting on a park bench pretending to read a newspaper.

As he drew close, she didn't look up or appear to recognize him. She just kept her eyes on the paper. "Sit down," she said. "Are you sure you weren't followed?"

56

"I'm sure," he answered, not looking at her. He wanted to get this play-acting over and talk to her normally. He waited for her cue.

Slowly she folded her paper and opened her purse and took out a cigarette. Then she turned to him and, as if seeing him for the first time, she asked, "Please, do you have a light?" He lit it for her.

"This little charade must seem ridiculous to you," she said, turning to him again, now more her natural self.

"I can only guess about it. You must have had a pretty good reason for being so secretive about our being seen together. What is it?"

She crushed out the cigarette with her shoe. "This tastes awful. I don't normally smoke, but it's a handy prop." She gave out a long sigh. "The problem is my mother."

"Does she know about us? Does she know who I am?"

"No. And yes. She suspects something. We had a miserable session. She read off Party discipline at me. I told you about my mother, didn't I?"

He said he remembered her saying she was a minor functionary of the Party here in Leipzig. "But why all the hush-hush?"

"I don't really expect you to understand. Just believe me. Mother is a good Communist. She has surrendered her total self to the Party. You must understand that, at least. If she suspects anything in my actions that is at all selfish, anything that doesn't serve the Party, it must be corrected. And she does suspect! After you phoned she quizzed me and boxed me in with her questions about you. She was horrified that I would meet any man from the Federal Republic alone. I told her I was working on you for the sake of the Party."

He thought for a moment and then asked, "Are you?"

"Please! Herr Hirn, I don't know what you think of me, but . . . ."

"Herr Hirn? After our . . . our . . . our moment up there

57

in the hotel room, I thought you would know I want you to call me Werner."

"No. That's too real, too personal — more personal than I dare to be. Let me give you a new name. What — oh, anything — how about 'Light'? That's good, isn't it? You've brought a kind of light into my dark world. Light . . . Lighter. How does it sound?"

He thought it sounded weird, but said, "Okay, if you like it. But you didn't answer my question. You're not working on me for the Party — I know that, for if you were, you certainly chose a crazy way to do it."

Lise looked down and examined her fingers. "You want some explanation as to why I risked coming to your hotel, meeting you here, and inviting you to Leipzig in the first place. Well, there is no explanation. At least none that fits the thought patterns that my indoctrination has given me. I'm not really a Communist, you see. Oh, I was raised as one, I wear the pin when I have to, I go to meetings of my group when I have to, but I'm a rebel. I've discovered that I have a self apart from the group. That's very dangerous. That's heresy."

Werner frowned. "I guess I should have done my homework. I don't understand everything you're saying to me."

"Of course you don't," she smiled. "But if you could only see that a meeting like this would be impossible, impossible for me if I were really what I'm supposed to be. I'm like a child, really. For years and years and years I've had it pounded into me that there is only one good — the Party. There is only one truth — the word of the Party; only one standard for right and wrong, for morality, for love, for marriage, for parents and children, for peace or war, for friends or enemies: will it serve the Party? The Party, the Party, the Party! I shouldn't tell you all this — how do I know that you haven't been planted by them to break me down?"

Werner was highly embarrassed by the confession he had

been hearing. He felt powerless to help her, to know what to say.

She continued. "I wouldn't be the first one to be trapped by the lure of independence and all that goes with it. But the Party has its apparatus for handling this problem, like everything else."

"How?" That's all he could think of to say, he was so confused.

"At the first signs of weakness and deviation they watch you and follow you and get reports on you and get the evidence on you and then you undergo the cathartic of self-criticism. You must purge yourself. And you do. The first time for me was —" She stopped. She shook her head again and again. "I can't tell you this! I must get a hold of myself. I've gone too far already! I can't run on like this!"

Her voice was choking with the pain of the mental lashing she was giving herself. She put her head in her hands. He thought she was crying, but he heard no sobs. He wanted to put his arm around her, but he didn't dare, not knowing what her reaction would be at this moment.

"Herr Hirn, let's get our business over with," she said, looking up at him with clear eyes, sharp eyes, cold eyes.

"But my name is Lighter, remember?"

"Herr Hirn, I've been a fool, and I apologize. I've entertained you, I think, and probably confused you thoroughly by my performance. I could go on and tease you some more. You're so naïve. I could have you all sewed up in almost no time at all. I could submit a little and then more and more and finally I would have you. Then I could build you and mold you and sooner or later you would be serving our Party, too. You would have no choice, as I have had no choice."

"What in the world are you saying, Lise? What is all this gibberish? Come, snap out of it," Werner said sharply.

"I have snapped out of it, don't you see? I'm letting you off the hook. It's very simple. You're free." She looked him straight in the eyes. If she had shown the slightest inner torment, as she had some moments ago, he could have stood it. But she was serious. He saw that she was serious.

"But what if I don't want to be free? What if I think you're just afraid, just playing a role in a script? What then?" he demanded.

"I would say that would be very unwise, Herr Hirn. Please try to face reality. If you don't, I'm sure you'll only bring trouble and danger on yourself. You've been nice to me. Let me help you to extricate yourself before you get in too deep."

He was stunned. He still didn't believe it, couldn't believe it after what she had told him. He *knew* she was just trying to restore herself somehow to the plateau of security from which she had slipped. Had her training made her a professional schizophrenic, one who was able to flip-flop on command from one personality to another 180 degrees different? But he felt that he had broken through the wall of her psychological defense, and could again. Of course she might have been out to trap him, to proselytize him for her cause . . . but why? Why? With a heavy weariness and with disappointment but no relief, he concluded that this was neither the time nor the place to pursue their relationship.

"Could I ask one last favor?" He decided he had nothing to lose by trying.

"Of course."

It was probably a dangerous thing to do, and might be a mistake, but he asked it anyway. "It's a personal thing. I'll probably leave the day after tomorrow. Maybe sooner, if I can. But I'd like very much to drive back to Berlin by way of the town of Freiberg. There are some relatives there I'd like to see for my mother's sake. If you are still in the good graces of the Party, perhaps you would put in a good word for me to get the permission."

Without hesitation she asked, "Have you applied through the regular channels?"

"Yes. I told them I wanted to stop by to test the Cathedral organ for some film recordings. They said it would have to be cleared with DEFA."

"With DEFA? Well, I know some of their people from Berlin who are down here filming part of the festival. If I knew more about it, I could try with them and see what happens," she said with her official radio-trained voice.

"I can't tell you any more than that," he answered. "And I wouldn't want you to get into any trouble over this. I just thought I'd mention it, as I do want very much to go. Perhaps it could even be to the Party's advantage to let me go," Werner added, not meaning it to be anything more than an extra thought for good measure. But her slightly lifted eyebrow seemed to say she read an implied threat into his words.

"And I have a last favor for you. A fair exchange, perhaps," she said, and nodded. "Please don't try to see me again. If anything comes of this from DEFA, I'll leave word at your hotel. And I would thank you if you would keep our secrets secret. Agreed?"

She got up and offered him her hand. He didn't respond. So she just smiled and turned and walked away. He watched her go. She didn't look back.

5

FEW THINGS WERE MORE IMPORTANT IN FRAU LEHMAN'S LIFE than the chance to meet some of the really big names in the Party and to fraternize with them. This evening was to be an especially proud one because she could bring Lise with her and introduce her as a voice of Berlin Radio International. It was almost as distinctive an honor as a Party medal. She chatted on and on about the wonderful honor it was to be in the Party and to share in the rewards of socialism.

Lise was surprised and relieved that her mother hadn't mentioned their previous conversation. Briggi had a single goal before her this evening and wasn't about to spoil it with scolding. Perhaps all Lise's fears about her mother's reporting her confession of wavering had been needless. Maybe Briggi had just been acting like a mother counseling her child. But still the warning had been effective. Lise didn't doubt for a minute that Briggi was capable of tipping off the secret police to watch her own daughter. Mother love was only a valid reality within the framework of Party loyalty.

Frau Lehman had changed into a green print dress with a little cape and was arranging her hair in front of the mirror. She heard a church bell toll and looked at her watch. "We can't arrive too early," she said, and flopped into an overstuffed chair and lit a cigarette. "Are you hungry?" she asked her daughter.

"No, not really. I suppose there'll be something to eat at the reception, won't there?"

"Oh, sure. You watch and see how one of these affairs is run. Everything will be perfect." She looked at her daughter as she finished dressing. "You know, you're really very lovely, Lise. A good figure, a nice face and smart clothes. I had a good figure once, but I went to seed after I reached fifty. I hope you'll use your charm tonight."

"What do you mean?" Lise asked, knowing quite well just what her mother meant.

"Just think who is going to be there tonight. Party secretaries from the leading cities, members of the Central Committee — this is your opportunity to make sure they know who you are and remember it."

Lise brushed her hair with determined strokes. "I don't want to throw myself at these people. They're all pretty well immune to the pushy type, aren't they?"

"They're not immune to flattery. And when a pretty young comrade makes them feel young and important and clever, they'll like it and may remember that you're worth watching."

Lise glanced at her mother in the mirror and said, "I don't care to be watched, thank you."

Her mother ignored that, stood up and pulled the wrinkles out of her dress. "Lise, listen to me. You've been floundering in your socialist responsibility. You told me as much. You haven't been aggressive enough. Tonight may be your opportunity to find a new outlook on your services to the Party."

"You mean I should let any big Party boss or any old uncouth pig use me as a plaything?"

"Why must you persist in looking at yourself apart from the socialist group? Why shouldn't you be used for a good purpose if it will serve the right ends? We're all used, one way or another, and can be thankful for every chance to do it nobly."

Lise was disgusted. She tried listening to her mother

through only those antennae of her mind that were for regimented and controlled thoughts. But other receptors to another part of her brain were still tuned in, and the result was irritating — like two broadcasts coming through on the same wave length.

"I suppose you'd be very proud if I went to bed with one of these distinguished comrades?" Lise asked. She had had this comment on her mind all through the talk and was a little surprised to hear herself saying it.

Her mother didn't seem shocked. "You know as well as I do that no comrade could have such a thing in mind. It's forbidden."

Lise shot back, "And you know as well as I do that it's done whether it's correct or not. If it can be rationalized as furthering the cause of socialism, it's done. Most of the time it's done first and rationalized afterwards. Don't forget, Briggi, I live in Berlin."

Her mother lit another cigarette and began shuffling the papers on her cluttered desk. "It all depends upon *why*, doesn't it? That's why I say, don't be a wallflower tonight. It may be your chance for greater Party service."

Lise felt like asking her mother if it was loyal Party service that was behind the conception of her daughter Liselotte some twenty-seven years ago. They had never talked about it and Lise knew practically nothing about her father except that he was supposedly a soldier killed in the war. But it seemed likely that there was something about the liaison between her mother and father that wasn't to be mentioned. She had felt cheated many times during her childhood because she didn't have a father like some of the other children. Of course she did grow up in a generation of many fatherless children because the war toll was fantastically high among the German soldiers and it left a gap in the working and farming class, to say nothing of the heartbreaking gap in families of all classes. That she had her fatherlessness in common with some of her classmates had made it just a bit less bitter.

They took a taxi to the reception at the Press Center. Many were arriving at the same time and a kind of traffic jam resulted. As they walked in the main entrance, Lise thought of her aborted meeting there with Werner. Or should she think of him as her *Lighter*? Or just as Herr Hirn? Or wasn't she supposed to think of him at all? That would probably be better, especially tonight. But he was still in the reserved section of her thoughts. She had been cruel to him and hurt him. But it would be best this way.

Frau Lehman moved into the thick of the reception affair like the old professional she was. Her daughter tagged along but quickly felt stifled by the succession of pedestrian remarks and the avalanche of clichés she heard as one activist tried to outdo the other in the game of pretending to have fun. Maybe this was really fun for them, thought Lise. But it wasn't for her. Did she know anyone here? The others from the broadcasting service wouldn't dream of coming unless they were forced to. If they had been invited they would have appeared to be most grateful in their response but would have begged to be excused because of some other official function. There were always enough functions to provide excuses if you wanted them.

Lise remembered one funny occasion when she was to appear as master of ceremonies at a quiz program in connection with the Berlin Film Ball. It had been a highly touted affair and all of the workers of one great shoe factory had been ordered to attend. There were two thousand seats to fill. Twelve radio and television artists were engaged. Eighteen waiters were employed to feed the multitude. Then came the embarrassment of the functionaries when only thirty brave guests showed up. But they had to go through all the motions of entertainment and eating anyway, and without comment. It was a fantastic experience, playing to an empty hall. Then, to top it all off, the radio report the next day spoke of the affair in glowing terms as the high light of the week's festival.

How many comrades had stayed home tonight? There were about one hundred and fifty people milling about in one room and a couple of hundred in another. Most of them seemed to be visitors to Leipzig, some obviously from other countries.

How many SSD security men were in this crowd? They had the place well covered, you could be sure. If she spoke to the wrong person too long, it might be reported. On the other hand, if she succeeded in gaining the interest of some important comrade, this would also be noted. She couldn't just stand there. Her mother had warned her against being a wallflower. So she glided through the group and picked up a drink from a waiter. She paused by the side of two men who were laughing loudly. She took out a cigarette from her bag and looked over to one of the men, with a silent invitation for a light, which he promptly produced.

Lise held out her hand. "Good evening, comrades. I'm Liselotte Lehman from Berlin."

"Berlin? So am I," said the short, heavy-set man who was still laughing nervously. "Wolfgang Luft is my name. And please may I introduce a comrade from Belgrade, Jaro Blatnik?"

She turned on her charm transmitter. "From Yugoslavia? How wonderful that you can be at the Fair! I think your country has many exhibits here, doesn't it? Wasn't it just this morning that I was admiring the fine publications your cultural ministry has produced? You must tell me about Yugoslavia."

Comrade Luft beamed with pleasure. "Our comrade doesn't speak German very well. But he understands most things, don't you, Comrade Blatnik?"

The blond Yugoslav laughed and nodded. "Yes, yes, I understand most," he said in his thickly accented voice.

Among those passing the threesome and observing the

smiles on all faces and the hearty laughter of the Belgrade comrade was Lise's mother, Frau Lehman. She smiled and said, "Good evening," to each of them and beamed approvingly at Lise.

The Berlin man invited her to join them at the long table where the food was piled high. They walked around and selected from the buffet the fish delicacies. Then they found a corner table near the orchestra. It was a little difficult speaking and their voices kept rising in volume. Comrade Luft plied Lise with questions about her work at the station in Berlin and she gave him back the answers he wanted — she hoped.

Whenever someone obviously important walked by, Comrade Luft would lean over and say, "The Party Secretary from Dresden," or, "The Deputy Chief of Justive," or, "The Third Secretary of Cultural Affairs." When the head of the People's Police of Saxony walked by, Lise looked at him very carefully. He was a heavy man in a bemedaled uniform and seemed to float along, possibly on the inspiration of too many drinks.

She thanked her companions for their courtesy to her and excused herself. She noticed how many people noticed her. Soon several came up to talk with her. All the waiters offered her drinks. Her mother came over.

"You see, my love, the word is being passed. Comrade Luft is very important and it was a great honor for you to be at his table. Keep it up," she said, patting her daughter on the arm before rushing on to join another clique.

Lise eased over to the Police Chief of Saxony. Again she took out a cigarette and looked to him for a light. "I don't smoke," he barked hoarsely, "so I don't have one. But wait." He snapped his fingers. Immediately an aide was at his side. He gestured toward Lise and a flame was produced at once.

"Thank you, Comrade," she said to the police chief. He just smiled. He was feeling his liquor. "It's hot in here, don't you think?" she asked him.

"Ugh, yes. Very hot, very hot."

"How about some air out on the terrace?" She took his arm and guided him out through the doors. It was not unobserved by the others.

They stood against the railing and looked over the city. She chatted on about nothing in particular and he seemed to like the sound of her voice. "What a busy man you must be during the Fair," she said.

"Too busy," he grunted. "But do you suppose those idiots in Berlin would give me another five hundred men? No! And I need them desperately. Can't have them, they tell me, because they need them for the Zonal patrol in and around Berlin. Huh! They have twenty thousand men there now and they still can't keep their own soldiers from jumping the Wall!"

He must be very drunk, Lise thought. No functionary would talk like this if he were sober. No one would ever admit there were defections to West Berlin from the border battalions, although all the people knew from the RIAS reports that an average of one guard a day escaped.

"Oh, then I'd better not bother you with my little problem," she said.

"Why not?" he insisted thickly. "To do something for a pretty girl like you would be a pleasure." He touched her cheek and patted it. She hated his hand on her. "All day I have said No! Maybe to you I can say Yes!" He let out a vulgar chromatic crescendo of laughter.

"It's such a little thing," she insisted. She told him that a visitor from Hamburg was in town. He was very important to their work. He will need a transit visa to drive from Leipzig back to Berlin by way of Freiberg. The visa bureau has rejected his application. "Is there anything you can do?"

"No problem," he announced. "Here, write his name." He gave her a card from his pocket. "I might forget by tomorrow otherwise," he said and laughed loudly again.

68

She quickly wrote: *Transit visa for Werner Hirn of Hamburg to go to Berlin via Freiberg.* He took it, crammed it into his pocket without even looking at it, and then patted her cheek again. She thanked him and took his arm and steered him back inside.

6

WERNER SAT IN THE PARK FOR ABOUT HALF AN HOUR AFTER LISE
had walked out of his life. For many moments he refused to
face the truth that she had gone . . . that she had been able
simultaneously to close one gate to her mind and open up another. He tried not to think at all. He looked up at the sky
and studied the clouds, crimson-tinged from the sunset and yet
heavy with impending rain. He looked up in the trees and
watched the branches dance in the breeze. He studied the
waddling ambulations of the pigeons on the stone paths and
watched them fly away when some pedestrians came by. He
closed his eyes and listened to the hum and roar of traffic.
And then finally he admitted to himself that he was in a
dilemma.

He got up and started to walk. Twilight was ebbing into
darkness. In the distance he saw the first flashes of lightning
expose in silhouette some tall buildings and a pointed church
steeple. The Church — that was a part of it too. Unruly
gusts of wind rumpled his hair. He kept walking.

Now and then he would stop to look in a store window.
Everywhere he saw the double "M" trademark of the Leipzig
Messe. What a saturation publicity job had been done! But
why not, when the State controlled almost every business
enterprise? He might have compared the prices with those
in the West and he might have observed that the stores

70

seemed abundantly full of merchandise, but he just looked into the windows and really saw nothing of what was there. It was just something to do and it really didn't interest him at all. He had a bigger problem.

The crowds had gone now. Some cars and busses and taxis continued to whiz by but there were few people on the streets. He was tired. He was weary. He needed sleep. But he didn't want to stop yet. He didn't want to stop ever. He had a compulsion to walk and walk and keep on walking. He could exist that way and be doing something and yet be doing nothing. He tried not to comprehend the fact of his extreme loneliness. It was aggravated by his being in this strange city in this strange country. His own land and yet not his homeland at all. He was a foreigner who understood the signs and the language but there was a new language, too, seen in the ubiquitous compressions of socialist lingo. *VEB* for the State's manufacturing collectives (the "People's Own") and the stores also operated by the State labelled always *HO*.

He walked in the direction of the old City Hall. The war had removed many landmarks in Leipzig but many others remained and would stay — old famous buildings whose tradition and architectural identification with the ties between both parts of Germany could not be removed except by demolition. The old revered City Hall had now become an exhibit area for Communist propaganda. They had changed the name of the world-famous Leipzig University to Karl Marx University, and had transfused the faculty with their own kind.

Big drops of rain began splashing on the cobblestones and sidewalks. Soon the sidewalk was completely waxed with a liquid film and the glaze of wetness bounced back the lights from the cars and street lights and store windows, making him squint. But he liked the feeling and the fresh smell of rain. He continued to walk. Suddenly, strong gusts of wind whipped down the streets as a prelude to a heavy shower. He stopped at a store entrance for shelter and watched the rain beat down on the pavement. Torrents swept along the edges

71

of the street carrying the day's dust and debris along down to the sewer.

The heaviest downpour did not last very long and, when the rain was coming down moderately, Werner put up the collar on his jacket and started out again. The rain washed against his face and there was something astringent and regenerative about it, as if he were sharing the tears of a whole land.

So it's over with Lise. Over in a moment's transition from despair to disciplined dogmatism, from pity to paradox, from intimacy to incredulity! Good-by, Lise. You were a fantasy from the beginning.

Shouldn't he be relieved? He had almost been burned. Shouldn't he now reciprocate with his own flip-flop and pretend it never happened? Couldn't he rationalize his being here in Leipzig as a normal and natural thing that would become only a memory after he started back toward Berlin and crossed back to freedom's side of the Wall? Did he need to wait for the cross-over through the checkpoint? Wasn't he free here behind the Wall? Suddenly he looked up and found himself outside St. Thomas Church. Light shone through the open door and music filtered out to him. He made no decision to enter: he just walked in.

A contralto voice was singing a plaintive Bach aria. The song was carried along from the front of the church to the back on the quaint and dutiful rhythm of a harpsichord and cello continuo. Then the sad voice of the oboe joined in with them to weave a strand of enchantingly haunting music. It soothed Werner immediately. He slipped into a seat on the aisle.

He looked up to the altar and saw the choir there and a small orchestra. He just let the music play upon him, not listening for the words. Then the steady beat slowed and came to a stop. His eyes followed the line of the aisle up to the front, past the tomb of the composer Bach, to the choir now standing for the final chorale. The strings announced the theme and then the voices poured forth their glorious paean of praise to God.

He remembered having been in this church before. It must have been during the war when he visited Leipzig with his parents. He looked up at the pulpit that met the people half-way down the church. He associated this with a remembered feeling of sanctuary from the chaos of war — bombs and burning and rubble and horror. Inside the church it was another world. Then, and now.

After a pause, the organ began to play. Instantly Werner thought of his father. His father had loved all the Bach chorale preludes and fugues and Werner knew many of them by name. He listened and recognized the powerful hymn theme of *St. Anne's Fugue*. He easily recalled the words, too. He had sung them many times:

> *O God our help in ages past,*
> *Our hope for years to come,*
> *Our shelter from the stormy blast,*
> *And our eternal home.*
>
> *Under the shadow of thy throne*
> *Thy saints have dwelt secure;*
> *Sufficient is thine arm alone,*
> *And our defense is sure.*

Werner followed the various organ voices as they picked up the theme of the great fugue and were blended together in a forthright testimony of faith. Help, hope, shelter — were these what faith was supposed to add up to? Is this what his father had found in the Church and had tried to express through his music? Was this music telling him this again now — that there *is* security and shelter and hope and help from this God of the Ages? Or was it only for the former times when his father had played the organ, when he had been confirmed? He wondered, If it is also for today and for years to come, why are there only five percent of the people in this town, in this land, who seem to believe it?

73

*If it is still valid, why don't I believe it? Do I believe it?
I do but I don't. It's good and true and nice but I manage
without it, don't I? Or do I really manage? Then, why do
I walk the streets of Leipzig alone and afraid? Is the faith
something I want, but not enough to fight for?*

*Fight? "Fight the good fight of faith." My verse. Mine.
But I didn't fight. I surrendered. And now is the battle lost?
Our Germany lost the battle and lost the war, too. But I grew
up in the wake of that war alongside the buildings that rose
to replace the ruins of a lost war. Where am I in all this?*

Only as the people began walking by him on their way out
did he become aware of the present: a man alone, cold and
wet, sitting in a shelter from the stormy blast.

Outside the rain had stopped. The stars were out. He
didn't want to walk any more. Where was a taxi? He wanted
to get back to the hotel and climb into bed and sleep off the
emotional weariness and spiritual confusion, and face life
somehow anew tomorrow.

At the hotel he went to get his key but remembered he still
had it in his pocket; this reminded him of his undercover departure. He saw something in his box. A letter. As the
clerk gave it to him, Werner looked at it for some clue. He
held it in his hand until he was safely in his room. Then he
opened it:

> *My dear Lighter — It's okay about Freiberg. I was able
> to arrange it. Don't ask how. Just see the head of the
> Saxony People's Police on Katherinestrasse tomorrow morn-
> ing, Room 218. Tell him you received word that he was
> able to give you clearance for a visa. If you ever come to
> my side of Berlin, look me up.*

74

7

THE ROAD FROM LEIPZIG TO FREIBERG WAS NARROW AND FULL
of curves. Werner needed frequent references to the map.
This was not at all like driving on the Autobahn. But he loved
to drive this little, responsive car; at least a car was something
he could control — better than his own heart.

On the radio some woman was talking about the Messe and,
for an anxious moment, he wondered if it could possibly be
Lise; but he found nothing familiar in the voice and concluded
it was not she. It started him thinking about her again. He
had all but abandoned the idea that she could still be a part
of his life. And then came the paradox of her note. Even
after all she had said, she still wrote to him using her name
"Lighter" for him. And she had managed the special transit
visa. And, most important of all, she had left the door open
for him to see her again. Why?

As he was circling through the rolling foothills of the Erzge-
birge Mountains toward Freiberg, he passed several huge
mining establishments. There was no sign identifying them
as such, but he knew from what Frau Dreitlein had said that
these must be uranium mines. They seemed fairly quiet
today. There weren't many workmen or cars or trucks about.
Perhaps the Russians had taken the uranium they needed from
this deposit and now the mines weren't working at the same
tempo as before. But he could tell that it had once been
a booming area.

He rounded a curve and there he saw the great Cathedral of Freiberg dominating the landscape. He would head for that place and inquire about Mrs. Dreitlein's daughter, the widow of Dr. Hans Spier. He knew she was a faithful participant in church activities, and doubtless someone at the cathedral would know where he could find her.

Another reason he wanted to go to the church was to allay suspicion. He didn't know what Lise had told the authorities regarding his interest in the visit to Freiberg, but his own application was still on file and it stated that he wanted to investigate the organ. So just in case they sent word ahead to check on Herr Hirn, Werner would play the game that way and would be safe.

There were a few people along the sidewalks and streets, but not many. Those whom he passed looked rather quizzically at the car, being obviously interested in the fact that it came from West Germany. The faces here were different from those in downtown Leipzig; he realized, of course, that to the Fair had come businessmen from all over the world and that those who entertained them were likely activists and persons in the favor of the regime. But here in Freiberg there was immediate evidence that the people had a hard life. There was deep anxiety in their faces. Everyone looked as if he had a perpetual headache that removed the luster from the eyes and brought indelible lines of concern to the face.

Around to the side there was a church office. He parked the car in a little parking lot in the rear and rang the church office bell. It might have been open but he didn't like just walking in on these folks. Better in this country to prepare people for visitors. He waited for a half-minute before the door opened. There stood a lady in the black habit of a deaconess. When he asked if she could help him find a family in the town, she introduced herself as Sister Sigrid and invited him in. They walked up a flight of stairs and into a little lounge area where there was a table and around it a few overstuffed chairs. A bouquet of fragrant sweet peas was on the table.

"Sister Sigrid, just so that you know who I am, let me explain that I live and work in Hamburg, and my mother lives in West Berlin. I have been visiting her there and had the chance to go to Leipzig for the Messe. I was able finally to get permission to drive here on my way to Berlin. By the way, in Leipzig I had a good visit with my former pastor, Dr. Moser."

She nodded, indicating she knew who he was.

"My father was organist in his parish in Dresden some years ago."

"What was his name? Hirn? Not Otto Hirn?"

"Yes, that was my father."

She immediately brightened and was obviously relieved to have received his credentials. Everyone in East Germany, he noticed, was instinctively circumspect in what he said until he knew exactly to whom he was talking.

"I have heard him play. In this church. You must meet our organist, Herr Walter Hendel. He would be proud to show you his famous instrument," she told him happily.

"Wonderful. It just happens that I told the authorities in Leipzig the reason for my wanting to come here was to evaluate your organ for a possible film recording. I don't know if that impressed them or not, but I thought it best to do what I said I would do — just in case they check up. Of course my real reason for coming is to find the family of Dr. Hans Spier."

Her face took on real sadness as she said, "Dr. Spier is dead."

"Yes, I know that. But I would like to talk to Frau Spier. I have a message for her from her mother. You see, my mother and Frau Spier's mother are close friends and neighbors in West Berlin."

Sister Sigrid looked at her watch. "I know the doctor's

widow and children very well. They are close to the church. It is not easy for them these days, let me warn you."

"I know that, too. Her mother told me. That's why the message is so important."

She explained that Frau Spier had been forced to go to work herself now that her husband was no longer there to support the family. She would not be home yet.

"Perhaps I can drive over there and wait for her," Werner suggested.

"No. I would not recommend it. It would perhaps cause more difficulties for her if she had a visitor from West Germany. The functionaries would find out about it — there is someone in each street and in each apartment building whose duty it is to report to the Stasi anything out of the ordinary. They would question her, perhaps, or claim that she was spying or something. Anything that would suit their purposes, whatever they might be. No, we must do it some other way."

Werner realized again that there was no freedom in the East to come and go and to see whom you wished without fear that it would have dangerous results.

Sister Sigrid had a plan. "I will go over there on my bicycle and tell her that you are here and arrange for you to meet. I think it would be safest to see her right here in the church."

"But I don't want to trouble you," Werner protested.

"This is why I am here. To help as I can. This would be best. It will not cause talk if I stop by. I do it often with those families that are having trouble," she said and added, "and there are many, my friend."

Sister Sigrid had another idea. She phoned for Herr Hendel and asked him to come over to the church to meet a visitor, the son of a famous organist. When Werner heard this, he felt proud of his heritage. He had never, to his knowledge, been introduced to anyone like that before. She announced that Herr Hendel would be right over and would meet Werner in the organ loft. She took him back there and they climbed the steps together. She suggested he wait there. Then she retreated to go on her errand.

Werner had been in many cathedrals as a sight-seer, and he had a general impression of them as dark and dank and meaningful only as museums reminiscent of an earlier day. This cathedral, too, was historic, but unlike the others, it was not dark but bright and radiant. It had apparently been restored in fairly recent times. It communicated a vibrant message through the strength of its art and architecture.

He soon heard someone on the stone steps. A tall, angular man appeared. His horn-rimmed spectacles and long white hair accentuated his artistic bearing. "I've been wondering who you are. Don't tell me. I know your father was an organist and let me see if I can see any resemblance from looking at you." Herr Hendel studied Werner's face for a full minute. Then his eyes twinkled and he said, "Otto Hirn. Otto Hirn? Could he be your father?"

Werner was delighted to know that the old man could guess. He had never been aware that he looked like his father, and perhaps he didn't really, but surely there must be a strong enough resemblance for this man to spot it. Werner answered his questions in general terms about why he was visiting Freiberg, and then asked Herr Hendel to show him the organ.

"Of course. Of course. You must see it. Do you know about this organ?"

Werner said he knew that it was a Silbermann organ and was considered to be one of that master's greatest.

"Greatest? Perhaps. Naturally, I think so and many others do, too. It is indeed the largest one he built. Did you know that the Master had his workshop and studio just a stone's throw from here?" He led Werner up to the console. Above it towered three rounded tiers of pipes, each section forming a kind of pillar of pipes, topped with a gothic cornice. The organist opened the doors to the console and proudly displayed his prize instrument.

"Do you play, too, like your father?" Herr Hendel asked.

Werner explained that he had always regretted not studying with his father. "But I'd like to hear *you* play."

"Certainly. What would you like? Of course it must be Bach, no? After all, this was built in Bach's own time and Silbermann was Bach's favorite organ builder."

"The St. Anne's Fugue?" Werner asked without hesitation. Herr Hendel smiled with satisfaction at the choice. Then he rubbed his hands together and pulled out the desired stops on both right and left banks. Werner watched with fascination. It was like seeing his own father in action again.

As he set the registration, the organist kept talking. "The organ is from 1714. Oh, I could tell you much about it, but I think you are most interested to know that your father played on this organ, too. I know. We have the records yet in our church. I could even tell you what he played."

Then came the familiar theme. For Werner it was like last night in St. Thomas Church in Leipzig. He turned and looked down at the church and his eyes were drawn to the altar. When was he last at the altar of a church for the sacrament? Years ago. Would he still be welcomed there? Would it be honest for him to go after all this time?

Fight the good fight of faith. This man with his music and Sister Sigrid with her deaconess service were doing that . . . fighting *for* the faith *with* the faith here where it cost something to fight for anything except Communism.

While Werner was still there listening, the deaconess returned. She whispered to him that Frau Spier would come to the church office directly after she came home from work. He could come up there and meet her.

Frau Hilde Spier came into the church lounge room and was introduced to Werner by Sister Sigrid. Then the deaconess withdrew, saying she would be available if they needed anything. She assured them they could talk here privately.

The woman had a poise and a smile that bespoke graciousness, bearing, intelligence and status. From her manner it

80

was not hard to see her as the wife of a very important doctor. But her costume made her seem miscast for the role. She had on a plain, blue, wrinkled work dress, a kind of uniform or smock. Her hair was wind-blown and somewhat disheveled.

"Please, Herr Hirn, forgive my appearance. I have just returned from the factory. When I got the message that I should come immediately to the church, I didn't wait to change or bathe. I knew it must be something urgent. Sister Sigrid had not told the children why I was to come. You see they might unwittingly report it in school tomorrow and the authorities would become suspicious if someone came all the way from West Germany to see me."

Werner was happy to tell her about her mother in Berlin. He didn't know much about her, but he expanded on the facts he knew — that she was well and healthy, and that she visited with his own mother every day, and that she was concerned about her daughter and grandchildren and wanted him to visit her. He decided to wait with the specific message he had been entrusted to deliver.

There was a knock on the door. Sister Sigrid came in with tea and a tray of sandwiches. She set it out on the table between them and then retired again from the room. Frau Spier poured a cup for Werner and then for herself.

"Your mother felt your situation here was very bad. Is it?" he asked. "Can you tell me about it?"

She thought for a moment. "Let me tell you a story. A true story. Then perhaps you will begin to understand.

"Eight years ago a tragedy happened in our family. The first of several tragedies. We had five children . . . then. My husband was the finest doctor in the city. While others fled to the West — in those days they could quite easily — my husband said No. He was a doctor. He couldn't desert his patients. He was needed here more desperately than in the West. We could get along. Oh, it wasn't because of his love for socialism or the police state. He was often furious at the regime here. But he felt his duty and we stayed.

81

"The officials had the policy then — and now, too — that doctors must be treated well. They couldn't afford to have them leave. Many left anyway, because they couldn't stand it. We stayed. We weren't bothered much. We had our fine house outside of town in a nice area. Also my husband had a kind of clinic in the center of the city and we had a small apartment there in connection with it. He had earned good money with his practice over the years and from his father's family had inherited many fine things of furniture and rugs and treasures. So we kept two homes.

"The children sometimes stayed at one house and sometimes at the other. On the day I am telling you about eight years ago — the day of the tragedy — two of the children were with me at the clinic. I was needed to help my husband there. Ursula was then ten and she was home with the two youngest children.

"There was a fire. . . ."

Frau Spier's eyes glistened with tears. She stopped and closed her eyes to gather strength to go on.

"Our house in the country caught fire. We never knew how. The children were inside. Ursula yelled for help. The neighbors said afterwards they had thought it was one of my husband's patients in pain, that likely the doctor was at home and so they needn't be concerned. But no one came and the house was burning. Ursula . . . poor Ursula . . . what could she do? The smoke was so bad that she couldn't reach Hans and Erika. She could not get downstairs and outside. So she was at the window of the second floor and the fire became so fierce that she jumped, with nothing to stop her fall but the ground. She broke her hip in the fall, but still ran to the neighbors and there she collapsed in hysteria. Hans and Erika died in the fire. . . ."

She struggled to control her emotions. She swallowed and resolutely continued.

"This I tell you, not so that you will pity us, but so that you might understand better about Ursula. She is a sensitive

82

girl. A fine musician like her father. She learned to play the flute beautifully. Well, the experience was sad and shocking and tragic for all of us, but particularly for Ursula because she felt responsible for the deaths of her smaller brother and sister. It wasn't her fault of course, but her heart wouldn't believe that. She had a real trauma from it — and sometimes still has.

"Later, after she had been confirmed, we sent her to West Berlin to a French school. We could afford it and we felt it was wise to have her develop her music and think about other things. Also, because she had refused to take the Youth Pledge and instead had been confirmed, her school opportunities would have been limited here even though she was a doctor's child.

"We could not get a new house but had the apartment at the clinic where we lived. Then came August Thirteenth. We had to make a decision. Should Ursula stay in the West or come back to us, not knowing whether she could ever leave here? The Wall was a frightening thing. We decided she must be with us and she returned home.

"After the Wall, things became worse for us. Oh, they still kept us isolated from political problems pretty much — not entirely — but my husband found his work increasing every day. At the hospitals it is a fact — other doctors will tell you the same — fifty percent of the patients have what the medics call the Wall-sickness. These are real ills — physical reactions from the heartache caused by divided families, almost complete loss of hope for reunion, and increased fear. My husband worked night and day. He never could get sleep. I worked hard, too, to help him as I could. And then he worked so hard he became ill. It was a brain tumor. It took his life. I was left with the three children.

"We had some money to go on and we were left alone for a while. But then things changed for us. Ursula wanted to study again in music and art as she had started in West Berlin. The officials, however, said No. She had been trained in Western ways already and was not fit for education in the higher schools of the DDR. This was a real shock and there was no appeal from it. It meant that her studies were over. Her hopes for a great career were all smashed.

"So it became necessary for her to try to get some kind of work. We wondered what she might do. In the West a young person from a doctor's family like ours is expected to prepare for some high intellectual or artistic profession. That could not be. Perhaps, we thought, she might try to get a position as a beautician or hair stylist or barber. We asked about it. It would not be possible, they said; such a work is open only to those who *deserve* it in the Worker-Farmer state. We thought perhaps of her becoming a masseuse. Again No. We thought and thought and asked again and again — about twenty different requests and every time the answer was No!

"Well, then, we asked them to tell us what she could do. They replied that she was eligible for only two things: She could make bricks and tiles for stoves and ovens in the kilns as a laborer there, or she could work on a collective farm — on an LPG farm — tending to the pigs and chickens.

"I tell you the truth, Herr Hirn. Ursula was so terribly upset and troubled that her old nightmares about the fire returned. She was a sick girl. She even stopped playing her flute although I told her she must, for her own soul's sake. I will not let her go to a collective farm. And I will not let her slave in the brick kilns. She is not strong enough for that. She is a sensitive girl and it would ruin her to do such things.

"So far I have been able to keep her at home. But it has meant that I must go to work. All right. I am willing, if I must, to work in a soap factory. Of course I am trained and able to serve as a medical assistant — not as a nurse but at least as a helper. But no — I could not get a permit. And the law now is that no one can change his employment without official permission.

"Forgive me, Herr Hirn, for going on so. I have had all

84

this pent up inside of me for so long and, now that I know you are here from the West, I had to tell you."

Werner assured her that he had come here for just this purpose — to learn what it was like for her and report to her mother. He was grateful for her speaking to him so frankly. "What of the other children, Frau Spier?" he asked.

She sighed deeply. She had given vent to her feelings and he felt she was getting weary. He was about to say that perhaps that could wait, but she had more to say.

"Helmut is fourteen. He is in confirmation class. To us church is important. How else could I have stood it when first my babies were burned alive and then my husband died? I realized then that there is only one source of strength and hope and love and that is Christ Jesus, my Lord. And I want this faith for my children, too. They know. They know what death means. And they can sing, as they do in church and at home, "*O Death, where is thy sting?*" and know what the words mean because they are Christians. But they also know what the Saviour meant when He said, *Take up your cross and follow me.* The children have been laughed at. Helmut would not join the Young Pioneers. He would not join the Free German Youth organization. He would not take the Jugendweihe pledge. So he must pay. He gets special work assignments, something every night until late. And Ilse, too. She is nine.

"Her teacher said that all of the students in the class must show how they are helping to build socialism. They must do something extra and report on it. The easiest way is through the Pioneers, of course. But I say No, and Ilse says No, too. But work for socialism they must. So Ilse thinks hard and figures out something. She will gather old bottles from vacant lots and alleys and places like that and also metal junk that the State wants to collect. This will be her contribution to socialism.

"The only time a child could find time for that would be around the supper hour when it's getting dark. Or after dark.

I am her mother and I said No. But the pressure was on Ilse at school. Then after I heard her weeping on her pillow at night and heard her crying out in her bad dreams, I agreed. It was the lesser of two evils. It is not right, Herr Hirn, not right at all. There is no time for them to play. They become filled with fears and worry about political questions at their age. You can see that they grow old when they are still babies — their faces tell the story."

Then she was spent. She had poured out her heart with an emotional freedom she hadn't known for years. But it took its toll. She began to sob and shake with utter weariness and grief. Watching her there, almost helpless to say anything or do anything for her, was for Werner a searing and painful experience. He stood up and put his hand on her shoulder. Perhaps even that would tell her that he cared. It did help. She was able to dry her eyes and mumble her apologies. He poured her a cup of tea which by now was only tepid. She sipped it long and thoughtfully.

"I think your mother is trying to get you out," he said, finally.

She heard him, but clearly didn't believe him. Then, she forced a smile, and said, "I'm afraid my mother doesn't know how difficult that is."

"Perhaps not," he said. "And I can't tell her all of this — it would be too much. But don't underestimate your mother. She is a determined woman. And there still are ways."

"What ways?" she said, with a sudden quickened interest.

"You've heard of the tunnels . . . and there are places on the border. Now and then with careful planning some can crash through."

"Too dangerous! I know the police and their methods. They will have sealed off all those channels."

He wanted to say something that would make her believe that it could happen. He wanted to ask her if she couldn't somehow have faith that it would happen. But who was he to lecture her about faith?

86

"I don't know what your mother will do, but I can tell you one thing, Frau Spier. I will help her. She will not be alone. If it takes money, we will get it somehow."

"Money?"

"Well, there is that new brand of artisans who specialize in escapes for a fee — two thousand, twenty-five hundred, or three thousand West marks — sometimes more."

She shook her head. "I don't understand how they can do that."

Werner replied, "I don't either. But I wish you would try to believe it can happen. You have faith in God. Pray that it may be possible for you to come out of the Zone, somehow . . . some way. And leave the way to — to us. It will give you something to fight for." And Werner, when he heard what he was saying, thought that it would give him something to fight for, too. Then he added, "Now, I have a special message for you from your mother about this."

"Message?"

"Yes — instructions. Listen carefully. Your mother, when she has made the preparations, will send you a simple birthday telegram. It will not be timed to arrive for anyone's birthday. But it will be a signal. You are then to take your children with you and come to East Berlin."

"I see. I understand. And then?"

"When you have arrived in East Berlin, telephone this number. It is a private party who will have information for you where to go with your children to wait." He wrote the number on a card and gave it to her. "And then, when you are settled there, wait for a contact from someone."

"A strange business, this," she said. "Oh, I have thought about it plenty. I have thought of writing to all those friends we have in the West. But I haven't dared to put my requests in writing through the mails."

He knew he shouldn't hold her any longer. She had her family waiting at home. And she was emotionally drained. He went to call Sister Sigrid. She came at once.

"We had a good talk," he said to the deaconess. Sister Sigrid looked at Frau Spier and sensed immediately the emotional exhaustion of the woman.

"I'll go back home with you," Sister Sigrid said.

"Oh, no, please. It isn't necessary," the widow protested.

Werner suggested that he could drive her home in his car, at least within a block or so. The deaconess agreed that this would be best.

Frau Spier told him where to drive and indicated where he might stop. Then, as she was opening the door to leave, she took Werner's hand and held it tightly. "Don't worry about me. Tell my mother I am thankful for her message and that I do understand. I will have faith. And with your faith and my faith, perhaps God in His mercy may have us rescued. And if we must stay, we'll bear that too, with His help. Thank you for coming to me. It is the answer to my prayers of each day. God bless you. Good journey."

8

WHEN LISE RETURNED TO BERLIN, SHE RESUMED HER WORK AT the radio station in the same routine manner, but her experiences in Leipzig with her mother and with her *Lighter* had left her utterly confused. She tried to put it all behind her, to forget about it. That private corner of her mind that she still reserved for her independent personality, however, was still alive with thoughts of him. The simplest thing was to conform, and conform she did. She took the copy that had been given to her for broadcast and read it over the air with conviction, as an obedient Party hack. Who was she to question the rationale of the Party for the line they chose? If she were called upon to write a speech for Comrade Ulbricht himself, she would be able to synthesize it with adequate dialectic phrases that she knew would be acceptable.

But perhaps Comrade Liselotte Lehman would not be permitted to put aside the memories of the Messe so easily. She had done her job well at Leipzig. The official with whom she had laughed and consorted at the reception was more than casually intrigued by her charm. He had taken the trouble to do a little profile on this attractive Comrade and he had her history before him. He also needed someone for a special assignment. He had a visitor from the People's Republic of Jugoslavia on his hands who wasn't being very cooperative. He wasn't revealing the information the Central

Committee needed. Comrade Luft would have to try more persuasive tactics. So he sent for Lise.

When the order came to report to the office of Wolfgang Luft at the Stasi headquarters, Lise had no idea what to expect. The SSD! She didn't give it too much importance, because the secret police could be involved in anything and everything. It wasn't unusual to be ordered to report here or report there to answer a question or fill out a form or meet a colleague for a special assignment. The discipline of the Party prepared her for anything and she had usually been able to take it in stride as another part of the day's work.

She arrived at the appointed time at Comrade Luft's office. From the size of his office and the crisp attentiveness of the secretaries and aides, she knew immediatly that he was a very important person. Naturally, she had to wait. Waiting to see people, to get papers approved, to be allowed to do this or that was part and parcel of life in East Germany, not only for the underprivileged, but also for the elite of the Party.

She was informed that she was to enter his office. In Leipzig this man had been a jovial sort with a smiling Jugoslav in tow. He had been in good form that night as a happy, lighthearted functionary. But today he was different. He was obviously not trying to be charming. On the contrary, he was all business — cold and frank and direct.

"Comrade Lehman, we have an assignment for you. It is a special work. And my information suggests that you are particularly interested at this time in co-operating with our security department."

Information? What was he referring to?

He saw her reaction and said, "Perhaps I should be more explicit, Comrade. We know that you have been exhibiting certain dangerous independent tendencies. You have pursued a deviationist course by attempting to establish clandestine contact with an unfriendly visitor from the Federal Republic."

"To try to persuade an uncommitted visitor to our State that he might find a cause here worth championing should

90

hardly be classified as deviationist, Comrade," she responded. So they knew about him, did they? But perhaps not his name or identity yet. But that would come next. She was familiar with the thought process being employed.

"Things would be a good deal easier if you would give us the full details. Such a potential ally — or 'uncommitted visitor' as you call him — should not be the sole responsibility of one person. After all, we are a collective society and the group is superior in its judgment, as you know."

"What do you want me to do?" she asked.

The functionary smiled. He had made his point and could afford to be affable again. "You remember the pleasant Commade from Yugoslavia, Jaro Blatnik? You met him in Leipzig. He is here in the DDR as a part of a trade mission. But that is only a cover. We need to know exactly who he is and what he wants here. So far, he hasn't been very co-operative. We are asking you to ply all your charming talents on this comrade and secure the real information."

"But, Comrade, I'm not an expert in this kind of intelligence."

He looked at her coldly. "You are a woman. You will know what to do. Of course, we will give you a little refresher course in security procedures, but most of this is routine for anyone with your training and social awareness." He pressed a buzzer. A small, balding man with thick glasses appeared at the door.

The chief introduced the aide to Lise and told him to give her instructions. As she was being escorted out, Comrade Luft gave her a parting warning, "You will, of course, co-operate completely. Your regular tasks continue as before. This will be an extra contribution to the people's welfare. Meanwhile, the evidence in your file will remain in my personal care and keeping."

The subordinate took her to another office far down the hall. Lise wondered just what "evidence" was in her file. Had her mother dutifully reported her daughter's heretical tendencies? She hoped not, but could not be sure. How had they known about *him*? Had she been followed during her meetings with him in Leipzig? Or had her actions that day on the Mügelsee excursion aroused the suspicions of her colleagues? Did they know his name and identity? Of course, she had introduced him. And how about her intercession for him with the police chief in Leipzig? She had been foolish to do that and give them direct cause to blackmail her.

The man had her sit down at a table and he began his routine of briefing her. First he read her a short profile of Comrade Blatnik. He had worked with the Jugoslav partisan group during the war, was a brother of a functionary in the early Titoist regime, had been Deputy Party Secretary in Zagreb for a while, had a wife there, and now traveled rather constantly for Tito as a trade representative without portfolio. It was essential to find out why, and what information he wanted here. "You may offer to get it for him," the man concluded.

He gave her a card with a number on it. "Memorize this telephone number and then give the card back to me. It is your contact for assistance or to report information that is urgent. There will always be someone there to answer day or night."

Then the man said matter-of-factly, "It is not likely that you will get this co-operation without giving your co-operation. You are to entertain him. He will naturally expect you to sleep with him."

She tried not to look as stunned as she felt. She hardly heard his instructions about the first date. She sat there in a daze, not knowing what to think. One part of her mind was filled with revulsion and she shuddered at the thought. The other part of her mind knew that this sort of thing was done and that it was all sanctified and guiltless if it served the Party. The tension between her two selves made her ill with a headache and nausea.

Once outside the Stasi headquarters, Lise just stood breathing in deeply the fresh air. She mustn't think of her sentence. It couldn't be! Perhaps there would be a way out. She mustered all her discipline to tell herself that she could contrive some plan to stave off having the Slav use her as a sexual pawn. If she had given herself completely to the Party, as she was supposed to do, this would be no problem. Whatever was then required by the Party would merely be an "honored duty" as an extension of the rite of self-immolation. But she had not surrendered all of herself. The reserve of individuality, which she held tenaciously, whispered to her that she was a woman, a sensitive human being, and that her person and her body were not intended for political prostitution.

She was due at the radio station. This new assignment was just an "extra contribution," as Comrade Luft called it. When she walked into the news room to pick up her copy assignments, her colleagues were laughing about something. She had interrupted the recitation of a funny story, obviously. The laughter stopped abruptly as she entered — merely a reflex action on the part of those who constantly must be on guard. She managed a friendly smile to the others as she went over to her desk and this relaxed the momentary tension. Lise gathered up her papers, accepted a policy memo that one of the young men brought over to her, and left for the seclusion of a small announcing booth where she could edit her broadcast material.

Her assignment was a report on socialist literature on the evening "Magazine of the Air." She couldn't seem to approach the problem with any freshness or creativity. Fortunately this wasn't expected anyway; within the routine of information broadcasts, it would even be considered dangerous. Automatically, and with well-trained detachment, she scanned the copy. There was a memo instructing her to report on a speech by Kurt Hager, Politbüro member and chief of the Central Committee's Ideological Commission. The twelve-page speech was attached. She would have to read it and make a pertinent abstraction. She had done this so many times under the pressure of the clock that it didn't faze her, despite her emotional distress. Lise knew better than to read every word. The speech would have few surprises. It would be Party line — it would have to be, or it wouldn't have come through to her desk. She scanned it, reading only the first sentence of each paragraph. It followed the form: Ample padding with the usual predictable recitation of dogmatic statements. She waited for the key words. There they were, beginning with "however. . . ." This was the meat of the speech. This was what she would quote. She began to type her script.

> *Socialist authors in the German Democratic Republic were warned today by Comrade Hager, head of the Ideological Commission, to keep themselves unstained from the modernistic and decadent influence of literature personalities in the centers of capitalistic decay and latter-day bourgeois decadence.*

So Herr Hager was spanking the literary heroes in Ullbricht's school of Communist writers! Why? They included several old-time Party regulars like Stephen Hermlin and Anna Seghers who had been cited by name. Lise had read their bold pieces written in the wake of de-Stalinization. They had demanded an "open art" and had all but rejected Communist realism. They had thought they were following the line. But then Khrushchev had reprimanded the "new wave" artists in the Soviet Union and now his puppets in the DDR would finally have to follow the leader.

> *Comrade Hager said that various authors are beginning to give themselves airs as though they were experts in political economy. They declare, he said, that the intellectuals and not the working class should be entrusted with leadership. Before they know it they will land exactly where the enemy wants them — namely in the camp of those who are the foes of rule by the workers and farmers.*

She typed out her script without any personal identification with the words she wrote. She ripped the pages off the machine and took them down the hall to the chief editor.

He glanced at the pages. A frown appeared on his face. Then a look of real astonishment.

"Where did you get this?"

Lise showed him the memo and the copy of Comrade Hager's speech. The man shook his head. He went over to a table and picked up a copy of a newspaper. "This was a close one. Look at this!" He handed her a copy of *Izvestia*, the Soviet Party newspaper edited by Khrushchev's son-in-law.

Her Russian was poor but she instantly knew the significance of what she saw: across two pages was a poem by Aleksandr Tvardovsky. For the past six months he had been in disrepute because his own writings were too liberal and he had championed other writers who had been criticized.

"They've reversed themselves again," she said, looking to him for confirmation.

"Exactly," he said. "Everything Hager said is today one hundred and eighty degrees away from the new Party line. Listen: 'The poet went to Khrushchev's Black Sea resort and read his new poem to the Premier.' What more is needed? But that's not all. This also says that the newspaper of the Union of Soviet Writers has been permitted to publish the speech of Ilya Ehrenburg who calls for 'greater experimentation by Soviet authors, and recommends that Russian critics read Joyce and Kafka and the French writers who have been recently called decadent.'" The chief editor was very excited.

Lise was surprised but not really surprised. It merely intensified her revulsion at the Party's duplicity. "What do you want me to do? Rewrite this with the new line? It would be a bit difficult."

The editor took her script and ripped it in two. "This is no good now. We will have to wait for some official in the DDR to make a pronouncement. It will come any day now, you'll see. You might as well go home. Thanks, anyway."

She couldn't get out of the studio fast enough.

Where to go? What to do? She wanted desperately to

talk to someone who could understand. There was no one. No one at all. A great wave of loneliness covered her. She could walk . . . and would walk. She had no destination. Walking was the closest thing to escape. Escape? Was she ready for it even if there would be a way? Others had done it, others who were desperate. Some had died in the attempt — or were now languishing in prison to pay for their crime in attempting desertion. Was it worth all this to her to try to crash through the Wall? What was life to her now anyway? She had known nothing — almost nothing — but an existence as a part of a social structure that owned her body and her mind and her spirit. The regime denied that there was anything like spirit or soul, but this was the one small reality that Lise knew beyond the regimentation of everything else.

Was this to be the final chapter of her life? Was it going to add up to nothing more? Was she being destroyed by the fact of her own mind's cruel dichotomy? What would she leave to the world? More of the emptiness that smothered it now?

She had never really faced death. It was not provided for in the Party discipline. None of its literature admitted death's reality. The heroes of the Party had set the example and did not even permit themselves to mourn members of their own family who had died. Nevertheless, for Lise, the mystery of death could not be rationalized simply as a cold coda to the rhythm of life. For life itself, in spite of all the scientific dogma of determinism which denied it, was still to her a mystery whose secrets lay only in the supernatural and spiritual realms beyond her experience.

The arresting bleat of a police ambulance speeding down the street broke in upon her morbid reverie. That same raucous wail, sounding for all the world like the cry of some wounded mechanical beast in a death plunge, had never failed to quicken her heart beat and tingle her blood. Its sound unlocked memories of war and Nazi SS troops and arrests in the night. She stood transfixed as the charging black hulk, ablaze with a blue flashing light, screamed toward her and swooshed by on its urgent errand. Where was she? Where was she going? Lise looked around for a familiar landmark or a familiar face. Among those that passed, it seemed as if every eye avoided recognition. They all wore the same blank stare that betrayed no emotion. These passers-by were among the many emigrés from socialist reality who now walked the streets of the DDR. The Wall had made their physical departure impossible; but here behind the Wall, they had found their only retreat in what people called the "inner immigration."

Lise realized now that she had unknowingly walked in the direction of the Cosmos Cafe on Karl Marx Allee where the young intellectuals gathered, the university students, the artists, who dared to mix with visitors from the West. That was the place where she had first met him, her Lighter. Had some unconscious hope that he would be there now drawn her toward the place? It was highly unlikely that he would find anything attracting him here now, after having been burned once. But how she needed *someone* to talk with — someone safe like Werner Hirn, someone who would not report her feelings. Someone to listen and share and understand. She wanted *him,* she realized. But the Wall was between them, perhaps forever.

In the cafe she found a table alone. It was a noisy place. Laughter arose from many foursomes, and through the chatter several languages filtered to her ears. Two young girls next to her were obviously Americans, one a bleached blonde, the other a redhead. Their American accent confirmed their identity. Lise could understand and speak English adequately and listened to them. They were students, exchange students. She was startled by the transparency of their conversation; it allowed her to know all about them. They made no attempt to disguise their feelings about East Berlin in contrast to West Berlin.

Watching them out of the corner of her eye and listening to them gave Lise a determined thought: *They will be going back, today to West Berlin. They can take a message from me to him.* With calculated casualness, she looked around the room. Was anyone here watching her? Was she recognized? She would take the chance.

Lise took out a pack of cigarettes from her handbag and searched for a light. She made a big effort to find one. She reached into her coat pockets. This was observed by the American girls.

"Would you like a match?" the blonde asked. She offered a packet of American paper matches and Lise took it and thanked her.

"Have one of my cigarettes," Lise offered.

"Oh, thank you, we have our own," the blonde said with a smile. "We prefer American ones."

"Do you live here?" the redhead asked.

"Yes, I do," Lise answered politely and lit her own cigarette, and walked over with the flaming match to touch it to their cigarettes also.

"Oh, please, not three on a match. That's bad luck, you know."

"I'd never heard of that. Do you have many such superstitions in America?" Lise sat down at their table. "Do you mind my joining you?"

They welcomed her, chatting about how Americans walk around instead of under ladders, avoid black cats in their paths, and toss salt over their shoulders when it spills. Lise was glad that they didn't probe into her life. They were too busy talking about how wonderful life was in America.

Lise knew she could trust these girls. They would enjoy carrying a message for her. If only they weren't too naïve. Would they talk about it to everyone they met?

"I have a brother in West Berlin," she said finally. "I can't see him any more, of course, because he can't come here and I can't go there. Would you girls do me a big favor and take a letter to him for me?"

The blond girl answered for them both. "We understand about this problem. We'd love to help. It isn't illegal or anything, is it?"

Lise laughed. "Of course not. It's just a family letter. But perhaps you better not advertise the fact you're carrying it. Someone might think you're a spy."

The girls giggled over this. Lise tore a page out of the menu book. She turned the page over and wrote a quick note on the other side. She folded it and wrote out Werner's name. For a frustrating moment she was afraid that she didn't have his address. Then she remembered he had told it to her, and she had written it down; but she had later destroyed it so as not to have on her person any evidence of his identification. She summoned up her powers of recall and finally reconstructed their conversation. She wrote, 57A Clayallee.

She watched them as they left the cafe for the U-Bahn subway station. Would it work? Would it bring him to her?

9

WHILE WERNER WAS STILL ASLEEP, HIS MOTHER HAD SCURRIED over to report to Frau Dreitlein next door. There was little advance information to share, but the very fact that Werner had seen Frau Dreitlein's daughter in Freiberg was enough to give hope to this neighbor lady. She wanted to come right over and wait for Werner to awaken, but Frau Hirn explained that he had returned very late the night before from his trip to the Zone. She insisted that her son should first have a good breakfast before telling them about his trip.

Out on the back terrace in the sunshine, Werner, after his second cup of coffee, thought back on his visit in Freiberg and worried about how he could tell the essential parts of this story to his mother's friend. Then, before he could develop any strategy, she was there. His mother ushered her out to the terrace and provided two more cups for the remaining coffee.

"Did you give her the message? Does she understand what to do?" Frau Dreitlein asked immediately.

"Yes, yes, I made sure she understood," Werner answered; "but I'm not sure she really believes that this plan of yours will work."

Her face became taut with determination. "It will work. It *has* to work. Let's not spend time wondering about that. Instead let's figure out exactly how it's going to be done."

Werner smiled a genuinely approving smile at her. "You're a courageous person, Mrs. Dreitlein. Really. And your daughter — she's like you, too, I guess. A remarkable woman. Remarkable."

Frau Dreitlein demanded to know all about his visit. She begged him to start from the beginning and tell him just how he found her daughter, what she looked like, what words were exchanged — everything. Werner had planned to give her an expurgated version of the conversation; but as he spoke and was prompted by her penetrating questions, he realized that there was no need to hide anything from this woman. She was clearly as strong as a rock. He told her the whole story.

"I've decided you need help, and even though I have only a couple of weeks of my vacation left, I want to do everything I can — not only for your sake and for their sakes, but for my own," Werner told her.

"God bless you for that," Mrs. Dreitlein said. His own mother's eyes were shining with tears as she nodded her head and said nothing.

"I have some time," he said, "and I have a car. And I have some contacts that might be helpful. But I'm afraid I don't have the money this will take, and I don't know how to get it."

"How much money? How much are we talking about?" she asked.

Before he could reply, the front bell sounded. Mrs. Hirn went to the door and walked out to the gate. She came back with a note for Werner.

"Two American girls brought this. They asked me to give it to you," his mother said. Curiosity was written all over her face as she handed him the plain unsealed envelope.

Werner hastily withdrew the folded menu sheet. It wasn't signed but he recognized the name of the Cosmos Cafe at the top and the Karl Marx Allee address in East Berlin. He read:

Dear Lighter: I need you. I must talk with you. Please forget about what I said in L. I'm on your side. Please come. I'll be here every day from 5 to 7. Be careful. Please come soon! Love . . . .

Werner looked up and saw both of the ladies studying him.

"What is it, Werner?" his mother asked. "Is something wrong? You look troubled."

Werner forced a smile. "No, nothing really. It just means that I'll have to go over to East Berlin this afternoon. I hadn't wanted to go again so soon because I thought I should work here on your — excuse me, on *our* project."

He thrust himself back into their immediate problem and stuffed the note from Lise into his pocket. At the same time he also pocketed her problem in his mind. He would think about it later. He could hardly ignore it.

His mother had an idea. "Couldn't you talk to your Uncle Klaus again? After all, he lives alone. Maybe the family from Freiberg could stay at his place after they come to East Berlin."

Werner protested, "Mother, you don't understand about Uncle Klaus. He lives in a restricted area near the Wall."

"I know that," she answered firmly. "Maybe it's close enough to the Wall so that from the basement of his house a tunnel could . . . ."

"You're dreaming, Mother," Werner responded impatiently. "No one can get into that area without a special pass. They'd never let strangers close enough even to visit. And how could Widow Spier and her children get official passes? As it is, the police will be alerted to their having left Freiberg suddenly."

Frau Dreitlein listened carefully to this exchange, looking at both Werner and his mother as each spoke. Then she said, "But see him anyway, won't you? Perhaps he can arrange something, some place for them. He's our only contact at this point. If he's willing to do that, then have him call my friend in Berlin — you know, the one whose

102

number you gave to my daughter — to be sure the family gets to the right place."

"How about your friend's house?" Werner asked.

"She has no room. She lives with her son and daughter-in-law and their family. Both of them work so she takes care of the children and is there all day. And they have a phone. But it wouldn't work for her to take anyone in. Not with the children there to tell everyone in the neighborhood."

Werner shook his head. "Uncle Klaus has his own problems. I'm not sure he can help. But, yes, I'll ask him."

Mrs. Dreitlein leaned forward. "Now about the money. When can you find out about that? And the tunnel?"

"What do you know about tunnels?" Werner asked her. "There must be other ways, too."

"There are tunnels — everybody knows about them."

"Including the Vopos on the other side," Werner said grimly.

"Of course. But that hasn't stopped their being built. Will you try to find out exactly how the system works? At least then we'll know if there is a possibility."

Werner promised he'd get to work on it right away. He excused himself and went to put on his jacket and tie. Then he went out to his car and drove down Clayallee toward the center of West Berlin.

Werner muttered to himself as he remembered the letter from Lise. *Why can't she leave me alone? Of all times to try to get me involved again! Just when for the first time in my life I've got something really important to do that she wouldn't understand or even appreciate . . . something totally against what she stands for. She certainly must be mixed up, poor thing.*

At a stop light, Werner reached into his pocket for the note and read it through hastily. *She called me by my special name. She ended it with "Love." She says she needs me. There is something pathetically urgent about the*

103

note. She must have been desperate in order to take the chance to send word to me through those American girls. Should I go to her? Can I possibly help her? And if I do help her, what then? She's still an exciting person to be with, but too much of a puzzle, too much of a chameleon, too mysterious, too dangerous for me! I'd be crazy to let myself get entangled in the kind of web she could spin. And then he remembered her frank admission to him in Leipzig that she could woo him and win him and trap him if she wanted to.

But in the note she had written: *"Please forget about what I said in L. I'm on your side."* Was this just another flip-flop or did she mean it? Had she cut the lifeline to all that held her to them, or was she still hanging on by a thin strand so she could pull herself back if she slipped again? Werner was more irritated than intrigued by her letter; but, even so, he was intrigued, he admitted to himself; enough so that at least he knew he would see her and find out what her big problem was.

He parked his Volkswagen in front of the RIAS building and went in to see Fritz Schumann. He was surprised that the attendant at the reception desk at the main entrance let him go right up to the third floor to Fritz's office. Weren't they at all concerned about possible saboteurs? West Berlin must be full of Red agents who might consider RIAS a prime target sometime to attack.

Herr Schumann was closeted with a visitor when Werner came to his office. His secretary asked him to wait and then she took in a note telling him of Werner's arrival. Fritz came out with her and greeted his friend warmly.

"How was Leipzig?" Fritz asked.

"Interesting. And a little depressing, I thought. When can I talk to you, Fritz? There's something I want to find out."

"I have a young fellow from the other side in my office right now. I'm about to interview him for a broadcast. He came here voluntarily this morning. Two nights ago he escaped from East Berlin."

"How?" Werner was terribly curious.

"He was a soldier on border patrol. When his sergeant was sleeping he made a dash for the barbed-wire fence and made it. Come on in and listen, if you like. I'll be through in fifteen or twenty minutes and then we can talk."

Werner was introduced to a young man in his early twenties, wearing a sport shirt and slacks and a new pair of sandals. His face was red with sunburn and his soldier-cut blond hair stood up like a brush. Werner went to sit in a corner and then listened as the lad told his story to Fritz.

There was a general conscription of young men into the People's Army in the DDR and this fellow had been in uniform only two months. He had applied for border patrol duty in preference to marine or air service, as he planned to escape to West Berlin at the very first opportunity. His chance came the second night he was out on patrol.

Werner found himself a little awed by this unlikely-looking hero — yes, a real hero who had risked his very life to reach freedom. If that sergeant had not actually been asleep, he would have been compelled to fire at the deserter.

Fritz explored the boy's background. His father had died in the war. His mother had married again and his step-father was a member of the Communist Party. This produced tension in the home and the boy was constantly in trouble with his elders. Had he told them he was going to flee? Yes, but they hadn't taken him seriously. His stepfather had told him to forget the idea — it would be impossible because of the excellent border guards.

What would he do now in West Berlin? Fritz warned the soldier against getting involved with the night girls that loitered around the bright spots on Kurfürstendamm. He explained that the East Zone government hired these prostitutes to lure back former guards who escaped. "Sometimes

105

they are successful," he said; "their goal is to arrange com-
promising situations to be used as a basis for blackmail."

Then Fritz opened a little portable tape recorder and
set up the microphone for an interview. His office was studio
enough. The recorder was a battery-operated, spring-wound
model. When Fritz had cranked it up, they began. Werner
heard this soldier say that he, among the many others on
border patrol, had listened regularly to RIAS. In this way
they discovered that others before them had made it safely
across. Over 350 of them who had been interviewed by RIAS
since the Wall had appealed to their fellow guards not to
fire at escaping civilians, in spite of their orders.

"Now, what's your special problem?" Fritz asked after the
young man had left and they were alone.

How should he ask it? "More of the same, I guess, Fritz,"
he said; "I'm also interested in this escape business. There's
a family over there I have to help get across."

Fritz shook his head. "Sorry, pal, but I can't help you on
that. Good luck, anyway. But you know our position. Those
of us in RIAS can't be in the business of smuggling humans or
anything else through the border; we keep the channels of
truth open but that's about it. Please understand that I'm
not just sloughing you off. Even if I knew how, I couldn't
help you."

Werner hadn't been prepared for this. He was depending
upon Fritz as his source of all necessary information on the
East-West traffic. Fritz noted his disappointment.

"The only thing I can do, Werner, is to give you the name
of some people who came through themselves recently. A
civilian couple. I don't know how they did it. We don't
ask. Most are secretive about it, naturally. It's public knowledge that this couple was here at RIAS two weeks ago and
gave us an interview which we broadcast back to the Zone."
He looked up in a black notebook the name and address and
wrote it out on a slip of paper for Werner.

Werner understood the limitations imposed on staff people

106

at RIAS, especially when Fritz showed him some of the vituperation in print that had been collected from the East German press, including many cartoons, that accused the American radio station of spying, sabotage, warmongering, and all sorts of provocations. Never was there proof, and the broadcasters at RIAS, most of whom were Germans themselves, were determined that none of the accusations should be given credence by careless acts of their personnel. But at least the name of this refugee couple was a hot lead and Werner wasted no time in following it.

He traced the route he had come from his mother's house. The address was on Hohenzollerndamm, which is actually an extension of Clayallee. He drove slowly until he found the number. It wasn't an apartment or a dwelling at all but rather a house that had been converted into a shop. He read the sign: H. G. WULF BUSINESS MACHINE SALES AND RENTALS. Was there a mistake? As he opened the front door of the store, a tinkling bell announced him. No one was in sight but presently a small white-haired lady came through a curtained doorway from a back room. There was no trace of warmth in her pinched face as she inquired what he wanted.

"I'm looking for a Herr Blume. I was told that he would be at this address."

She was silent for a moment. A quizzical look crossed her face. It was enough to tell Werner that he had come to the right place. "Perhaps I can get in touch with him for you," she said, finally, "if it's important. Or maybe I can help you. Did it have something to do with a machine, or . . . ?" Her voice trailed off with a question mark.

"I think he can help me," Werner said. "I'm willing to pay for the information if he can give it to me. You see, there's a family on the other side and I have to get them over here." He realized that he had to be direct about this. They would be cautious about seeing anyone and talking about their escape. In their eyes he could just as well be an agent from the DDR trying to trick them into returning.

"Who are you?" the lady asked him, still with no trace of a thaw in her face or eyes.

"My name is Werner Hirn. I'm from Hamburg. I'm a good friend of Fritz Schumann of RIAS." Werner felt a twinge of guilt at using Fritz's name like this, but he told himself he had only made a factual statement.

Suddenly the curtains to the back room opened and a middle-aged man came in. He had a dark blue repair man's apron on. Obviously he had been listening to the conversation. "I am Blume," he said and came up to the counter.

Werner repeated what he had told the lady. The man nodded, seeming to understand. Then he had a few mumbled words with the white-haired woman and, in order not to appear trying to overhear them, Werner turned around and looked out of the window for a few moments.

Herr Blume spoke to Werner. "Come with me, please."

They went out the front door and followed a flagstone path around the building to a garden in the back. There was an entrance there to a basement apartment and Herr Blume knocked, then opened it with a key, and said, "A moment, please," to Werner. He went in alone and shut the door while Werner waited among the flowers. Then he returned and ushered Werner into the small living quarters.

Herr Blume introduced his wife. Her round face was all smiles. She had a faded blue dress that was a little too tight and revealed the contours of her plump form. They invited Werner to sit down. They questioned him about his work, his reason for being in Berlin, and his background. He included the fact that his father had been an organist in East Germany. Without revealing the city or the names, he described the doctor's widow and her plight and how he had promised to help them come through. All he wanted from them, he said, was the name of someone with whom he

108

could arrange for their passage through a tunnel. Could they help him?

The man said, "This is extremely delicate and risky business, as you know. I am not at liberty to give anyone the name of the person who made the arrangements for us. You can understand that. But I'll be glad to get in touch with him and explain what you've told me, and then if he will see you, I'll let you know."

Werner emphasized that he was hoping there wouldn't have to be too much of a delay. His vacation would be over soon and then he wouldn't be able to do much more about this. He was devoting himself during these two weeks to this problem.

"Tomorrow morning I should have the answer for you. Say about ten o'clock. Can you come here? I'll see this person tonight if possible."

Werner was pleased. His search was bearing fruit. He felt that he was making real progress. He thanked the Blume couple and said he'd be back the next day.

Now it was time to go over to East Berlin, on the other side of the Wall. He wouldn't take the time to return home to give his mother and Frau Dreitlein a progress report. He knew the process of clearing the border inspection might take a while and it was already mid-afternoon. He was hungry. Eating at a restaurant always consumed so much time — Germans love to have their meals leisurely. Perhaps he could stop at an *Imbiss,* the new eat-and-run stands patterned after American snack bars. But he really didn't have the appetite for a Bratwurst or a Bockwurst plastered with mustard. Instead he found a fruit market and bought some grapes and bananas. He brought enough to take some to Uncle Klaus also, and at the same time picked up some packages of cigarettes both for his uncle and for the Vopos on duty at the Wall.

Werner wondered if he should try the Bornholmerstrasse passage through the French Sector north of the Brandenburg

Gate. It also was reserved only for West Germans. He had never used it and really didn't want to experiment now, so again he headed for the same Heinrich Heinstrasse pass where he had crossed before. Actually he was nearer the Allies' Checkpoint Charlie but, of course, that wasn't open to him as a West German.

He was surprised. There were just a couple of automobiles waiting on his side of the Wall. The West Berlin police passed him through quickly. Then, as he sat waiting for the cars ahead of him to move, he ate his lunch of grapes and bananas.

Werner counted the money in his wallet while he waited. He still had about thirty East marks left from his Leipzig trip. He tucked them into one of the wallet's inner compartments. Should he declare these together with his West marks? Would there be complications if he did? Would there be problems if he didn't? He tossed the car registration papers on the shelf below the windshield and got his passport ready. He paged through it to the last entry. The transit visa permitting his travel to Berlin from Leipzig via Freiberg covered a whole page.

When the barrier pole was lifted by the Vopos on duty, he drove on through and parked in the designated area. He tossed a pack of cigarettes on the seat and went into the barracks building for the clearance formalities. The attendant took Werner's passport and glanced at it casually. When he saw the last page, he raised his eyebrows and wrinkled his forehead. Quickly he looked up at Werner and then turned again to the first page that contained his photograph and vital statistics. "Wait a moment, please," the official said as he left his stool and disappeared into a back room. He returned with another uniformed man who came out in the hallway with Werner's passport in his hand.

"Are you Herr Hirn?"

"Yes."

"Please come with me."

110

He led the way. Werner followed past the staring tourists and the money checkers to a side room. The official closed the door. The room was bare except for a table and several wooden chairs. With his hand still holding Werner's passport, the young man indicated that Werner should sit down. Werner tried to act casual but it was almost impossible to camouflage the nervous tension that gripped him. His throat went dry and his ears felt hot. He knew as soon as he came through the door that this was not routine. He had noticed those interview chambers in this building on previous crossings. They had always been vacant with the doors open. Now he was inside and the door was closed.

"Would you empty all your pockets, please. Place the contents here on the table." It was an order. The voice of the official was not patronizing nor polite. Neither was it sharp or caustic. Just a flat, matter-of-fact order.

"Would you mind telling me what this is all about?" Werner demanded. In his mind a rapid montage of reasons toppled over one another in a cascade of memory flashes.

"If you have nothing to hide, there will be no problems. We are merely doing our job," was the only answer he got. "Now, if you please, take out everything in your pockets and place it on this table." He rapped his knuckles on the bare table top to punctuate his order.

Werner hesitated only a moment and then began with his wallet. The main question in his mind was: *What do I have with me that might get me into trouble? My address book? No, fortunately I left it at home. The name and address of the Blume couple I just visited? Yes, Fritz had written it on a card . . . but where was it? In which pocket? Will that get me into trouble? The note from Lise! THE NOTE FROM LISE! They mustn't see that. I'll have to do something about hiding it — or can I just leave it in my pocket? Will they search me, too? And then if they find I left it there, will it seem even more incriminating?*

He concentrated on each item he felt in his pocket. He

would stall for time and then take out his keys . . . and then his handkerchief . . . his comb . . . the cigarette packs for his Uncle . . . coins . . . dark glasses. Then finally he felt he had no choice and took out the folded menu card from the Cosmos Cafe with Lise's note on the back. He held this in his hand and from another pocket took out the card from Fritz and a receipt from the fruit market. He put these down on the table with the fruit receipt on top.

The official looked at the array of items. He picked up the wallet and peered in each of the pocket compartments. He took nothing out. He shuffled the papers and spotted the menu. "What's this?" he said, picking it up and looking at it strangely.

Werner swallowed hard. "A cafe here in Berlin where I enjoyed myself the other night. I took the menu as a souvenir and thought I'd go over again today. Good food. You should try it sometime."

The official smiled ever so slightly. He put the menu back on the table. *He hadn't turned it over!*

"Now. Will you please take off your clothes." The official erased the smile. He leaned back in his chair and took out a cigarette.

"But why?" Werner protested. "Is this really necessary? You can search me with my clothes on."

The official merely leaned forward and rapped his knuckles on the table again.

Werner took a deep breath and exhaled slowly in a sigh. He took off his coat and put it over the chair. He loosened his tie. The official leaned back again, watching, and lit his cigarette.

Desperately he thought: *I've got nothing to hide in or under my clothes. This won't be so bad. But just so he doesn't examine that stuff on the table more closely. Let him leave that menu where it is. Why . . . why . . . why are they doing this? What was it about my name that made them single*

112

me out? Am I on a list? They must have some kind of
SSD report from Leipzig . . . or is it the special visa that
made them curious . . . or is it something about Lise?

"Everything? You want me to undress completely?" Werner
asked, standing there only in his underwear.

"Take it all off, yes," the man answered with absolute im-
passivity.

Up until now Werner had been too worried about what
this procedure meant, what it was leading to, to become
impatient or angry. Now, standing there completely naked
before this man, he found himself fighting for control against
a welling up of bitterness and disgust. *Why don't they tell*
me what they have against me? What possible purpose could
they have in humiliating me like this? Do they think I'm a
spy? Did they expect to find secrets taped to my body?
Maybe they want to scare me off . . . give me the works so
I'll not come back. Well, it's working. I won't go through
this again for anything!

He said nothing. He knew that any more protestations
at this point would only make it more difficult for him. The
official got up and slowly walked around Werner, inspecting
him.

"All right," he said finally. "Put on your clothes. And
wait here."

Werner got dressed. Faces and places from his two weeks
on both sides of the Wall flashed through his thoughts, each
faradizing a new current of emotion: alarm — fear — infatua-
tion — pity — disgust — anger — trust — doubt — self-possession
— self-delusion . . . .

He waited. He waited some more. Finally, the man returned. He asked a few perfunctory questions. Then Werner was released. Dismissed. Cleared.

10

AT THE COSMOS CAFE THE VIOLINIST, CELLIST, AND PIANIST IN gypsy costumes played a Hungarian dance. Werner sat at a table by himself, tense and alert, watching and listening for a moment. He wished he could relax and let the music quiet his turbulent spirit. He thought of ordering something to drink, but he was waiting for Lise.

He studied the patrons of the Cosmos Cafe. There was a kind of restraint among them that was markedly different from the five-o'clock crowd in a Hamburg or West Berlin cafe. The room was devoid of any suggestion of luxury or intimacy. The lights were bright. All the tables and chairs were tan colored; the chromium trimming and white-and-red checkered tablecloths gave it a proletarian accent. Perhaps the huge portrait of Ulbricht above the musicians' platform further discouraged excessive merriment.

A waitress came and placed a menu in his hands. He shuddered as he saw the familiar page with the Cosmos trademark at the top, matching the sample he already had in his pocket. He said he would wait for his guest before ordering anything.

He had intended to stop over to see Uncle Klaus first, but the weird ritual at the Wall had taken so much time he decided instead to find out first about Lise. It was already after five o'clock and he had expected her to be waiting for him. He watched every customer that came in, but he still

114

didn't see her. Had she changed her mind again? Maybe something had happened to her. Her note had sounded urgent and fearful. Could there be any connection between her difficulty and the frightening interrogation this afternoon?

He felt a curious pathos for her as he saw her in his mind. Lise had stunned him when she summarily broke the circuit of their affection in Leipzig. Like the suspended echo from successive swells of unresolved harmonic dissonances, his feelings about her and for her lingered disturbingly in his mind. He wondered if he could ever again think of her as an appealing woman. The enigma of Lise nevertheless continued to have a kind of gravitational pull for Werner, and he suspected it was more than mere curiosity or pity. He insisted to himself that the polarity between them was not love and could not be. But if not, what then was it?

He became aware that a man was standing at his table. He looked up and saw a waiter there. The waiter leaned over and asked softly, "Herr Hirn?"

"Yes."

"I have a better table for you. Will you come with me?" He smiled knowingly at Werner.

Werner followed cautiously. He was still on guard — his afternoon's experience of following a man who also called him by name had made him especially apprehensive. They went out through a back door to a terrace where there were other tables but no customers. The waiter led him across the terrace, through the lines of tables, and over to a little flower-box hedge at the far end. He motioned to Werner to walk around the greenery.

"I think you'll like this table. It's very private," the waiter said, smiling.

There sat Lise.

"Hello, Lighter! Thanks for coming."

The waiter remained standing there. Werner gave him a tip and waved him away.

Then they were alone. Lise, behind her mask of poised

115

self-assurance, looked as frightened as she had in the Leipzig hotel room. Her mouth smiled, but her eyes — those penetrating eyes he remembered — blinked nervously; her eyelids seemed held open by invisible props. They sat there silently for a moment, neither knowing just what to say.

"You look tired," he said.

"No sleep, I guess."

"Has it been rough?"

She nodded. "Can you forgive me for the way I treated you in Leipzig?"

"Forgive? You said it was for my own good. You helped me make that side trip. I have no complaints. I learned something . . . ."

"About me?"

He shook his head. "No, mostly about myself. I learned that I was selfish, living only for myself with no purpose except having a good time."

Her tired eyes searched his. "And now your life has a purpose?"

"The beginning of one, perhaps. I don't know. I'm a little mixed up right now."

"That makes two of us." She looked down at the table and watched her finger trace invisible designs on the tablecloth. "I'm in trouble. Real trouble. I need your help. You're the only one I can talk to. The only one on earth. I know I don't deserve even to call you my friend after . . . after what I did to you."

"You were afraid. I understood that."

"I'm more afraid now. I simply don't know what to do. I swear to you I won't pull away . . . . I won't hurt you again . . . if only you'll help."

He felt the web beginning to close in on him again. And yet it would be cruel and inhuman to abandon her at a time like this when she was so obviously distraught. But could he be sure? He knew that she was perfectly capable of playing him for a fool . . . of using him. But he had come this far.

She needed him. Now. He believed her. He needed to be needed.

"Tell me about it," he said. "I can listen. How else can I know if I can help you?"

Their waiter had returned. He cleared his throat and they looked up. Did they want to order something? Werner looked at Lise. She shook her head. Werner explained with a smile that they would wait a bit longer, if he didn't mind.

"I can't talk here. Can't we go somewhere where it's really private and safe?" she pleaded.

"Would we be followed?"

"You never know. You never know. But it's worth the chance — at least to me."

"There is a place," he said, "the only safe place I know in East Berlin. A church. Ebenezer Church. My uncle works there as the custodian. I have to go and see him tonight anyway. Let's order a meal now. You eat yours when it comes. I'll go on ahead in my car and park it outside the church near the side entrance. When you're through, in about an hour, you follow in a taxi. Walk the last couple of blocks. You'll recognize my car, the green Volkswagen. I'll leave it open. Wait for me inside the car."

She agreed, and after they had summoned the waiter and ordered a light snack, he stood up to leave. He reached in his pocket and took out the menu page with her note on it. He scribbled the address of the church on it and gave it to her. She reached for his hand and kissed it over and over again. Werner put his hand under her chin and gently tilted her head back so their eyes met.

"Don't worry," he said. "You're not alone any more."

At Ebenezer Church he found his uncle getting ready to lock up for the day and leave for home. He immediately sensed from Werner's nervousness that this was not the same kind of casual visit that he had made last time. There was something urgent behind Werner's coming.

"I need your help, Uncle Klaus. You're the only one I know

117

who can arrange things for us here in East Berlin. Tonight will be my last trip over. I've got to leave it in your hands."

The old man's face became very grave. He bit his lip. "What's happened, Werner? What are you up to?"

Werner explained about his trip to Freiberg for his mother's friend, about the situation that made it essential that they try to get the doctor's widow and her three children out, and about how he had promised, at the prodding of his mother and Frau Dreitlein, to arrange for this family to be passed through a tunnel.

"And is this possible? Do you have it all worked out?" Uncle Klaus asked.

"Not quite. There are many problems yet. But I need to find a place for them to stay, to hide, until the zero hour. That's where you come in. Mother thought you might be able to keep them at your flat, but I explained to her that no one could get into your neighborhood and into your building without a special pass."

"That's right. And there's a curfew, too. If I don't leave here soon tonight, it'll be dark and that will be bad for me," the old man added.

"Could you figure something out? Please. Would you try?" Werner pleaded.

His uncle bit his lip again and again and began pacing the floor. He stopped to look at his watch.

"All right. I don't know where, but I'll work on it. There are many things I cannot do. I try in my little way here to help our church so the people's faith in God can stay alive. It's a small thing I do. I've never been asked to do anything really important like this. Maybe I won't do it right. I'm not an educated man like your father was. But your mother is my sister and you are her son. You're trying to help someone to a new life. I guess I can help, too. Maybe that's why God put me here. I'll ask Frau Wilm if she can take them at her place or find one somewhere else. She was my housekeeper until — but I told you about that."

118

Werner hugged his uncle in a spontaneous gesture of thanks. He explained carefully that the Freiberg family would leave for Berlin when they got Frau Dreitlein's message and would telephone a pre-arranged number in East Berlin when they arrived. Uncle Klaus should make sure to call that same number to tell them exactly where the widow and her family was to stay. On a scrap of paper which he tore off the fruit-package wrapping he wrote out the number. The old man looked at his watch again and said he couldn't delay any longer. He had to leave. Then Werner remembered about Lise.

"One more thing, Uncle. Someone is coming to see me here. We need a place to talk privately. May I use the church?"

He didn't answer right away. He was pondering over this new question that required a decision immediately on the heels of the other. He picked up the package of fruit and held it under his arm. Then he looked at Werner and said, "Why . . . sure. If you're careful and keep the door locked. And if you leave all the lights off . . . and if you're quiet. I really shouldn't do this. Pastor wouldn't like it. But because it's you, I trust you." Silently he shook hands with Werner. Before he left, he showed Werner the night lock with its extra latch.

Werner looked out at his car in the street. There was nothing to be seen of Lise. It was already twilight. He hoped his uncle would make it home before dark. He went back inside the church.

In the dark corridor he had to feel his way to the sanctuary door. As he opened it a soft, rose-colored glow from the huge stained-glass windows enveloped him. The pews and the statuary and the pulpit and the choir loft were just faintly discernible in the darkness beneath the windows. With each step the floor creaked, and the sound seemed amplified in the empty church. The nostalgic odor of old varnish was a special kind of welcome. He sat down in the front pew. His eyes automatically focused on the place where the altar was, but in the deep shadows all he could see was the gleaming reflection of light from the gilded strips that framed the altar and the painting above it. As his vision gradually became adjusted to the darkness, he was able to distinguish the words carved into the altar *Come Unto Me, All Ye Who Are Weary.*

He closed his eyes and ran his fingers through his hair. Everything prompted him to loosen his soul in this place: the unspeakable beauty of this temple that was bathed in the softness of its private sunset . . . the magnetic invitation from the altar . . . his own mental and spiritual weariness. But could he pray? It had been so long since he had allowed himself to frame the words and thoughts of real prayer. And yet, he still believed, didn't he? He *had* known the reality of prayer. He closed his eyes and concentrated. The memory of Pastor Moser standing at the altar came to him and he heard him say the words — his special words — *Fight the good fight of faith!* Frau Spier's earnest face looked at him and he heard her say, *I will have faith. And with your faith and my faith, perhaps God in His mercy may have us rescued.* His uncle's words tonight returned to him, adding still another echo . . . *I guess I can help, too. Maybe that's why God put me here.*

Werner held his head in his hands. He found himself silently speaking the words, "Our Father who art in heaven, hallowed be Thy name . . . Thy kingdom come . . . Thy will be done. . . ." What *was* God's will anyhow? That he should help smuggle a woman and three children under the Wall? How would he know? Did it matter as long as he could pray the words and mean them: *Thy will be done . . . ? Help me, God. Help me to do what is right. Forgive me for . . . .* Forgive? Lise had wanted him to forgive her. He hadn't committed himself on that. Lise! She might be outside now in his car.

He opened the door and peered through the darkness out into the street. He saw his car but couldn't tell whether or not she was in it. He left the church door standing open and walked out to the street. There she was, waiting.

"Come inside," he said almost in a whisper. "It's okay now. We'll be alone." He took her by the hand and led her in and bolted the door. They went into Uncle Klaus's quarters. He told her that they would have to leave the lights off. In the darkness he found a couch and suggested she sit there. He pulled up a chair and sat down too.

"Now," he said. "Now you can tell me about it."

She said nothing. He heard only some sniffs that made him realize she was on the verge of weeping.

He moved over and sat down by her. He put his arm around her tenderly. "Lise, my dear," he whispered in her ear, "you're safe now. Let me help you . . . or at least try to help you. But I have to know about the trouble that's upset you so much. I can guess, of course, but you're kind of a puzzle to me and I might guess wrong. Take your time. Just rest here. No one is rushing us. No one is watching us. We're alone."

He felt her sobbing against him. He didn't say more. He thought of so many things he might have added for comfort and hope but he realized that the kind of words and prayers that might reach the hearts of others in a similar situation would not mean much to Lise. Words of faith and hope and love would be empty for her because those very concepts were foreign. He could try, but his heart told him that he could speak more effectively through silence. His protecting arms could express better what she needed to hear. And then she became calm. She straightened up and found a handkerchief in her handbag.

"I don't deserve this. I said that before, and it's true. You're too . . . too good for me. Thank you. Thank you, my Lighter."

He could feel the smile now in her voice.

"Oh, what a mess I'm in," she sighed. "Poor dear, you've been wondering what in the world hit me. I've been a problem for you. Well, here it is, in a nutshell: I've been forced to work for the SSD!"

"The secret police?" A chill went through him.

"Yes. The Stasi . . . the security boys have caught up with me."

"What does that mean, exactly?" Werner asked as calmly as he could.

"It means that they know about *you*, for one thing," she answered.

"I thought maybe they did." He briefly explained about his interrogation at the checkpoint on his way over.

"It was foolish and heartless of me to ask you to come at all. It could have been much more serious for you this afternoon. But I was frantic. You were the only hope I had. You must forgive me. And they are blackmailing me now. I have to work for them under the threat that they'll pull me in if I don't. Prosecute."

"What do you have to do for them?" He had a sudden fear that luring him over to the East Zone might have been part of the price she had to pay.

"I'd better not tell you. It's very distasteful to me. No, that's putting it too mild. It's revolting, really. It has made me see the rottenness of the Party and all it stands for."

"Does your assignment have anything to do with me?"

She turned quickly to him. "Oh, no . . . no. You didn't think that —? Oh, darling, no! It's something else . . . a special assignment. I'll try to get out of it if I can . . . . I'll get sick or I'll dream up something."

He put his arm around her again. "How can I help?" he asked.

"You already have helped. You know you have. And I don't deserve to ask for more."

"I want to help if I can," he added.

She stood up. She walked back and forth in a little arc. Then she turned to him and said, "I want to leave. I want to get out. I know it's almost hopeless, but I'm desperate,

122

you see. I've even considered killing myself. Yes, I have. But something deep, deep inside me held out for life. That's why I sent for you. Somehow, someway, maybe you can help me get to the West."

"Whew!" Werner stood up and went to her. "It's terribly difficult, Lise." He immediately thought of his exploration of the escape systems. All the problems that had already surfaced formed their own wall against the hope and determination she had. Of course, if he could include her with this family from Freiberg, maybe that would be a way. But he couldn't mention that. He didn't dare jeopardize their lives by telling Lise about them. After all, she was working for the Stasi, even though it was under protest and duress. They had ways of wringing information out of their agents.

"Do you realize how far I've come in my thinking this way?" she asked. "This means that I've really cut the umbilical cord. I can't get back to the Party's protective womb again. I've been born for the second time. The world is spanking me. And I'm crying. But I'm breathing free air already. And, for the first time in my life, I think I really know what it means to be loved by someone . . . someone who sees me as a single human being, not just as a part of a functioning group. And I am beginning to know what it means to love in return."

Suddenly she threw her arms around his neck and desperately found his lips. The shock set up a resistance in his body, a resistance in his own lips. But the warmth and genuineness of her outpouring of herself melted him and he pressed close and yielded.

"I'm sorry," she said as she pulled away.

"Don't be," he replied.

"I didn't mean to give you the wrong idea. I asked you to help me and here I go flinging myself at you, as if to say that you can have my love as part of the payment. I didn't mean that."

"And I didn't think that."

There was an awkward period of silence. She went back to the couch and sat down. He remained standing.

"You want to get out. And you think I can arrange it. Any ideas?"

She said she had wanted to slip into the back seat of his car or under the seat, but she knew that had been tried too often, that the guards now even looked in the trunks of cars and behind the seats. She had entertained ideas of getting someone to crash a truck or a bus right through the Wall. That had been tried, too. She had hoped that someone might be able to find an unguarded place in the fence extension of the Wall surrounding West Berlin. She had thought of disguise, of forged papers, of travel to Sweden or Poland or Finland or Austria or Czechoslovakia. None of these seemed at all possible. Then she asked, "How about a tunnel?"

"It costs money. More than I have."

"How much?"

"I don't know. I'd have to find out."

She said she would try anything to raise the money needed. She had absolutely no idea how, but it would give her something to concentrate on.

"I'll try, too," he said. "I can't promise. You know I can't promise. But I want to help if I can. But how can I get word to you? I don't dare come back."

She shook her head over and over again. "It's going to be so hard. But if you have news for me, try some American students. I'll be at the Cosmos as often as I can in the early evening. I'll try to use Americans again as couriers for me, too, if I have any news for you. I wish I could give you some hint on a broadcast, but I never know when I will be reading on the air and every word is checked by a censor."

"But at least if I listen I might hear your voice that way. After all, unless we do get you across, I may never see you again."

"Don't say it . . . don't say it. I will come. I will."

Then she stood up, knowing their meeting was over. It

124

was time to leave each other — perhaps forever. In the darkness he reached for her, then held her and kissed her tenderly. He couldn't let her go. Suddenly he clasped her tight, wishing desperately that the Wall had somehow crumbled and that she could be his forever. To love forever.

11

IT WAS GOOD TO BE BACK IN WEST BERLIN, WERNER THOUGHT.
But how strange the divided city looked spread out on the
map before him in the front seat of his Volkswagen. He
saw all of the main spokes of the traffic arteries leading to a
hub that was formerly the center of Greater Berlin, but now
that hub was in the East Sector behind the Wall, and many
streets that had once drawn the population to the city's center
simply ended at the barrier. Although each half of Berlin
had long since adapted to the exigency of division, and had
gathered its social and commercial life around new vortices,
the map told its own story. After exploring the labyrinth of
streets on the map of the unfamiliar Charlottenburg section,
Werner pinpointed the address of the tunnel builder, Herr
Braun, given to him by Herr Blume. He took his bearings
and drove right to the street without difficulty.

It was a bright sunshiny day. The leaves on the trees were
just beginning to lose their verdant green and were gently
dappled with yellow. West Berlin was a neat, prosperous
city and this street might have been any residential area in any
city. Perhaps in the dull gray of fog or rain, the weather
would better have evoked the mood of intrigue that belonged
to West Berlin, but today it was hard to reconcile the drama
he was experiencing with the invigorating cheerfulness of the
morning.

He found the right number but was surprised to discover

126

it was a modern new apartment building. He hadn't known what he was expecting but he somehow hadn't visualized the builder of a tunnel living in quarters so commonplace as this tall, sleek apartment house in front of him. Herr Blume had told him nothing about the man except his name and address.

As Werner rang the bell, his pulse quickened in anticipation of this meeting which would answer the fateful question: Could he accomplish this bizarre rescue that he had set as his goal? His ringing was answered with a buzz that unlocked the door; he entered the vestibule and searched for the man's name among those on the mail boxes. Fifth floor. He started climbing the winding stairway up to his rendezvous. Before he reached the top he heard a door open.

"Hello. Are you Herr Hirn?"

Werner was relieved to have the identification established immediately; he went into Herr Braun's apartment with the feeling that he was really being welcomed. He had rather dreaded this meeting, thinking he might have to convince the tunneler that he wasn't an intruder.

His host was a man of lively expression and quick movements. His eyes sparkled with delightful vitality. The bushiness of his hair accented the vitality of his personality. As he led the way into a living room, he walked with a bouncing step. There was no rug on the floor; the room looked bare with just a few pieces of furniture. Herr Braun quickly pulled up the nearest chair and invited Werner to sit down. He sat also, but immediately was on his feet again and left the room. He was very youthful. He couldn't be more than twenty-five, perhaps only twenty-two. In a moment the man returned with his wife, a young, delicate-looking girl.

"This is a very nice place," Werner told them. "You are fortunate to have such a fine apartment."

Herr Braun explained that he and his wife were students at the Free University. They became eligible for these quarters only because they were married University students.

Werner decided to go right to the point. Herr Braun looked at him with his wide eyes inviting a discussion of the business he knew Werner had on his mind. The recitation of the plight of Widow Spier and her family became an easy task as the young fellow gave his complete concentration to Werner's every word.

"And how does it happen that these people are a special concern of yours? Are you related to them?" the young man asked.

Werner told them of his work in Hamburg and how he had made a trip to Leipzig and had visited the Spier family at the special request of his mother's friend. He told them that it was really this personal encounter with the woman and her problem that made him determine to try everything possible to get her out.

The man looked at his young wife. There was a brief moment of silent communication between them. Then, when it seemed as if they had reached an understanding, he turned back to Werner and said, "I think you have come just at the right time." He looked back at his wife for reassurance. In her face there was agreement.

"I can tell you that a tunnel is being built right now. We've been working on it for two months. We hope to have it finished in a couple of days."

The words, when Werner realized their exciting significance, had a beautiful sound.

"You realize, of course," Herr Braun continued, "that this is very tricky and risky business. Every time we start to dig we're taking an awful chance. We have to be extremely careful to make sure that our plans and activities remain top secret. But I'm sure I can trust you. I wouldn't have let you come here if I hadn't been sure. I took the precaution of checking everything Herr Blume told me."

He looked again at his wife. "We have had visitors who were only probing for information. We didn't know why they came. Maybe they were trying to scuttle our plan or, even

128

worse, to trap us and those we were trying to rescue. So we're very careful."

Werner asked whether the publicity about the tunnels had caused much difficulty.

"Yes, of course. But most of the publicity came after we had already taken out several hundred refugees. You remember the TV shows. Well, I knew about those. That publicity helped, actually. It helped us get some of the money we needed."

"How much does it cost to build a tunnel?"

"It all depends upon the circumstances and the location. It costs more now than at first because the Communists have added over a hundred yards to the original ten-yard 'no man's land' on their side of the Wall. But a tunnel today may take fifteen or twenty or even thirty thousand marks — sometimes more. Sometimes we have to build two tunnels at the same time, side by side. One of them is used merely as a decoy while we rescue the refugees through the other. There have been times, though, when a tunnel was discovered and no one got through. But the costs had to be paid, just the same."

Werner asked what the most expensive part of it was — the digging or the materials.

"Most of the digging is volunteer work. Maybe you'd like to spend some nights digging for us!" He laughed and then became intense again. "The biggest expense is securing the right building, whether here in the West if we dig from this side, or in the East if from there. You see, none of the dirt can be hauled away. Every bit of it has to be stored in bins that fill six or seven rooms of the basement of the building where we work. If we hauled it away, it would reveal our secret right away. Most of the money is used to rent basements that are large enough and near enough to the Wall. There is some major cost also for the lumber we need for shoring up the sides of the tunnel to be sure it doesn't collapse. The tunnel we're working on now is taking fifteen tons of wood, five thousand tons of steel track for the carts that haul the dirt — this, plus electric power lines and motors and pumps."

Werner was vicariously participating in the tunneler's adventures. He saw himself plotting the steps necessary to undermine the "Wall of Shame" as Berliners called it. He asked, "Do you start from both ends and try to find a meeting point somewhere in the middle?"

The man laughed. He shook his head. "Oh, no. The digging is all in one direction. We end up against the basement wall on the other side. It is really difficult to hit the mark. That's why I am studying engineering at Berlin's Free University. I get good practical experience with my homework." He laughed again.

Werner was trying to calculate what it would cost to get Frau Spier and her three children across. That was his first problem. He must also find out what it would cost to get one more person through. Couldn't he include Lisa in the bargain?

The tunneler explained: Twenty-five hundred marks for an adult and half of this for each of the children. Werner quickly figured this to be six thousand, two hundred and fifty marks for the Spier family. And for Lise, an extra twenty-five hundred marks!

How much time would he have? Werner said that he hadn't been able to arrange to get the money, not knowing how much was involved or if a tunnel passage was even possible. He wanted to get to work on it right away. If he succeeded, where would he bring the money and how was it to be paid? When would it be needed?

Herr Braun explained that it would have to be in cash and it would have to be deposited with him at least twenty-four hours before the breakthrough. This was scheduled for Saturday night, if all went well.

That meant that Werner had only two days to round up the money for the Spier family and, hopefully, for Lise too.

130

He thanked them and said he hoped he could report back very soon.

At the door Werner turned to Herr Braun and said, "Tell me something. Why are you in this business? There must be some special reason why you're willing to take these risks."

The tunneler put his arm around his wife and said, "I lived there myself and I know what it's like. Before the Wall I used to go back and forth, studying here and living there. Then came August Thirteenth. My wife was over there and I was here."

"And did you build a tunnel for her?"

"No, she was my first refugee; but she came over, not under the Wall. We worked out a fantastic scheme and fortunately it was successful. One day some of my friends and I went to the Wall with 'Molotov Cocktails.' We threw them over at two different places about one hundred yards apart. This caused a great commotion on the other side and the Vopos immediately went to the points where the trouble was. My wife was ready. Quickly we put up a ladder between the two places and she scrambled over. Naturally, we couldn't repeat that. One thing led to another and soon we were digging underneath the Wall . . . and that digging has allowed over a thousand persons to reach freedom!"

At noon Werner's mother invited Frau Dreitlein over to eat with them. They sat out on the back terrace. Werner reported on his findings, including the most important item, that it would cost DM 6,250 to bring Frau Dreitlein's daughter and three grandchildren through a tunnel. The other important fact was that the breakthrough was scheduled for this coming Saturday night. They would have to decide how to let Widow Spier know in time for her to come with her children to East Berlin.

Frau Hirn was upset. "Where could we possibly get all that money?" She shook her head. She seemed ready to abandon the whole project.

Werner found the reaction of Frau Dreitlein to this news interesting. This amazing woman was certainly dauntless. She admitted that she had no bank account and no immediate prospect of raising all that money. Nevertheless, she insisted that there would be a way. She told them, "Money or not, I'm going to send a telegram to my daughter. A Happy Birthday greeting. If she's on her way to Berlin, we'll have to find the money."

Werner wondered about a loan. But how could it be paid back? Was there any other organization that had funds for such a thing? No, Frau Dreitlein had already investigated. Was there any individual who would have the means and some reason to put up the money? Werner wondered if he could ask some of his friends, but realized that one had to be a very good friend, indeed, to make an advance or a loan of this size.

Suddenly Frau Dreitlein jumped up. "Where's the telephone book?" she asked.

Werner's mother hurried to get it.

"There *is* someone. I think he might be a real possibility. I wouldn't dream of asking him for money for any other purpose. A man here in Berlin owes his life to my daughter's husband. During the war when Dr. Spier and my Hilde were living here in Berlin, they risked their own lives to rescue a doctor friend of theirs, a Jew. He was a marked man. His name — oh, what was it — it started with S. They kept him in their home. They hid him for weeks and finally helped him to escape to Sweden. I'm sure he hasn't forgotten. He is now an important doctor here in Berlin."

She turned the pages where the doctors were and quickly went down the alphabetical listing to those whose names began with S. Her finger traced the names until — "Yes. This is it! Dr. Lothar Schwarz." She held her finger at his telephone number and announced, "I am going to call him this minute and ask if he will talk to me."

Frau Dreitlein made an appointment and Werner gave her

a ride over to the office. En route they stopped at a post office where she sent the birthday telegram to her daughter. Her only fear was that the telegram might never be delivered.

He parked his car and went in with her to the doctor's reception room. They found several other persons, obviously his patients, waiting for him also. They sat there for almost an hour. Never once did Frau Dreitlein seem weary or discouraged. Her determination and confidence shone in the way she sat there patiently with her hands folded. Was she praying? The question prompted Werner himself to close his eyes and try to pray. He couldn't find the words, but he did experience at least the feeling of prayer; he hoped and he believed that God understood what he wanted to say.

The doctor's assistant came to Frau Dreitlein and said that the doctor would see her. Werner waited. He would have loved to eavesdrop on the conversation, but this was Frau Dreitlein's moment.

Only a quarter of an hour later, the door opened from the doctor's office. There she was with her face wreathed in a big smile. Werner caught a glimpse of the white-coated man shaking her hand and thanking her for coming. She didn't need to say a word to Werner. He knew. He wasn't surprised to see in her hand the doctor's personal check.

12

LISE PRETENDED TO ENJOY THE MUSICAL AT THE METROPOLE
Theater. Every inclination within her protested at the very
idea of her being there as a part of the entertainment bill
for the Comrade from Belgrade, Jaro Blatnik. She had rehearsed the possibility of evasion of this task but the stage
had been set too well.

The SSD had thought of everything: A car to bring them
to the theater, tickets to one of the best boxes in the house
where they were surrounded by other comrades (how many
of them were assigned to watch them?), reservations for a
theater supper after the show, and her own "entertainment"
suite in a government apartment building.

She had no choice but to play the clown for him and for
whatever special audience was watching her performance.
The entertainment on the stage was a much-touted modern
musical comedy, the first of its kind attempted by the DDR's
repertory group at the Metropole. It was a mild harpooning
in song and dance of bourgeois dress styles in the extreme
with the Leipzig trade fair as the setting of most scenes.
A few weeks ago, Lise could honestly have enjoyed this —
the authors had even been allowed to satirize through
double entente some of the socialist sacred cows. But she
had changed, and so the production's weaknesses were a
source of embarrassment and irritation. The music was not
original in character but rather sounded like a hodgepodge

of imitations all the way from Offenbach through Gershwin. There were few subtleties of lighting, and very little freshness in the staging.

Comrade Blatnik did not have to pretend to enjoy himself. He was delighted at the transparency of the action that could be followed even with his poor understanding of the language. He laughed heartily at the slapstick action and applauded enthusiastically after the songs and dances. His inhibitions had been loosened even before he had arrived to call for Lise, and she had been quick to note the pungent odor of liquor that enveloped him in the closeness of the automobile transporting them to the theater.

She wore a kind of mask with a frozen smile as she sat there looking at the stage. But she really didn't see the action or hear the lines and lyrics. Through her thoughts paraded possibilities for the delaying strategy and diversionary tactics she would need later when she would be expected to entertain with more than smiles.

Lise was aghast at his capacity for liquid stimulation. At the supper afterwards, he downed four cocktails to her one; she didn't dare go beyond that because she wanted to be completely in control of herself. At the apartment, the ever-efficient SSD had installed a bar. Should she keep plying him with drinks in the hope that he might collapse in a drunken stupor and thus leave her alone? Or should she divert him from the bottles so that he wouldn't become dangerously animalistic and brutal?

She surveyed the suite of rooms. It was lavish by official proletarian standards — a large living room with divans and thick rugs and a high-fidelity record player, a terrace and dining room with a small and compact kitchen, a bath, and a bedroom with one large bed. How many listening devices had the Stasi placed in these rooms? Was all their conversation being auditioned? She found some records and began playing them as loud as she dared.

Would talk, just plain conversation, satisfy him for a

while? Would she be in trouble if she didn't fulfill her primary assignment and get the information from him that the SSD wanted? If she were successful at that, would they censure her for not yielding to his advances?

Maybe she had him pegged wrong. Perhaps he wasn't really interested in using her for self-gratification. Would he forego any aggressive intentions if she got him to talk about his wife and his children? Or would this make him pursue her more?

Never before had Lise been in a quandary like this. She was caught in a vise of fear that could easily lead to panic. No man had possessed her. She had always successfully avoided the kind of encounter that could require a decision as to whether to yield herself or not. The most tender response she had ever permitted herself was the impetuous kisses she had given Werner. *Oh, dear, dear Lighter — will I ever see you again? Can't you rescue me now from this hellish nightmare?*

Her mind was operating on two levels. While the one was desperately calculating and scheming for a way out, the other was maintaining a flow of words and gestures to keep the Yugoslav entertained. As he listened to the steady rhythm of her German — she knew he couldn't understand it all and that didn't matter to her — Comrade Blatnik continued to drink. The records flopped into place and the music, with her chatter as a counterpoint, seemed to keep him mesmerized on the corner of a divan. He had his shoes off and was feeling no pain.

A gay song with a Latin beat brought him to his feet. "Let's dance!" he suggested.

Lise knew she had to humor him. He held her firmly and tried fumblingly to make his feet follow the syncopation. She tried to ease away from him and hold him at arms' length. He pulled her close to him again and stumbled through clumsy attempts at dancing. Then the record stopped. The next disc was a slow, dreamy ballad. His cue.

He became relaxed, and with flaccid fingers caressed her neck. When his hand stopped to grab the collar of her dress, all Lise's senses cried out in unison and she froze. Then in one impulsive stroke he ripped the zipper down, all the way down, and pulled at her dress until it fell to the floor.

She tried to scream but no sound came. *What will he do next? Will he completely disrobe me? I've got to get away . . . but how?*

He reached for her again. His big hands grabbed her wrists. Instantly, in one wild move, she tore herself loose and swung at him, slapping his face again and again and again.

He didn't flinch. His eyes merely opened wide in incredulous shock. When she stopped and backed away, he rubbed his mouth and looked at her in disbelief.

Lise snatched her dress and dashed for the door. She flung it open and ran out into the hall and down the stairs. She didn't stop until she had reached the landing two floors below. He wasn't pursuing her; she was safe for the moment. Slipping her dress on, she moved down the remaining stairs to the ground floor.

Her mind was flooded with fear. Her breathing was panicky. *Was the house being guarded by the security men? If I walk outside, will I walk into a new trap? But I have to take the chance.*

A man was there near the door as she had feared. She didn't stop to think. She acted only on impulse. She gestured for him to come over. "Up in Apartment 4A. A man up there. He needs help. He seems ill. Will you go right up and see if you can do something for him? Call a doctor if you think it's best. I have to go and report to headquarters right away. Please do what you can!"

He went. And she hurried down the street, not knowing where she could go or hide. Fortunately there was no traffic on the streets. Everything was deserted. She walked block after block without being seen. Then, finally after

137

what seemed like hours of intense walking, she saw the lighted sign of a U-Bahn subway station. She went down the stairs and looked around. On one wall she spotted a train schedule. The hands of the clock were at 1:30. No trains until 3 a.m. Dejectedly she mounted the subway stairs again to the street.

She didn't know where she was. But she knew she had to keep walking in the direction away from the apartment house. Dazed and weary, she didn't even try to assess her fate. She knew only that she was still safe. Inevitably she would be pursued. *Keep going . . . keep going.*

Taxi! There ahead of her she saw a taxi with its welcome light on top. Would a taxi be safe? It had to be. She would have to take the chance. She got in and asked the driver to tell her the nearest U-Bahn station where the trains were still running. He said he thought it would be the Alexander Platz Station.

"Good. Take me there, please."

The driver nodded. He started up his engine. Uncertainly he looked back at Lise and asked, "Excuse me, Fräulein, but are you in trouble or anything like that?"

She didn't answer. She didn't dare say yes, and she didn't have the strength to deny it.

"I guess I am," she said finally.

Immediately, he started up the car and drove down the street. "Can't I take you home? Wouldn't that be better than going to the station at this hour?"

"I . . . I'd better go to the station. I'm afraid to go home, actually."

He drove on in silence for a few minutes. "Excuse me, but what will you do at the Alexander Platz Station, if you're not going home? Sorry to ask so many questions, but I'm worried about you. You look as if you've just been through something that pretty much upset you."

"Yes, you're right. A man tried to rape me, that's all."

138

She felt like crying but knew she must hold on and control herself.

Again the driver was silent, as the cab rolled through the darkened streets. "If it's that bad, and if you're afraid to go to your own home, you are in no condition to be left at Alexander Platz. What will you do there? Sit on a bench until dawn? No. You're coming home with me."

She shook her head, protesting.

"Don't get me wrong. I'm taking you home to my wife. She'll know what to do. Anna will take care of you. And don't worry about our saying anything to anyone. It will be our secret."

13

IN THE SUNSHINE OF THE NEXT MORNING, LISE WALKED PAST Ebenezer Church and a half block beyond it. Then she turned and retraced her steps. She paused at the open gate and read the notice that announced the weekly schedule of matins, vespers, and Sunday worship services. She looked over at the side door of the church for some clue to help her decide whether she really should go in. What would her Lighter think? She walked past the gate and along the sidewalk in the opposite direction.

Wouldn't he want her to come here for help if he really knew the danger she was in? They hadn't made any such plans. She couldn't be sure that Werner understood how desperately she meant it when she pleaded with him to help her escape. How could she have told him then what was behind her fears? Even now, could she possibly describe to him the terror of last night with that man? She had tried to blank out all thoughts of it, but it was still too close, too real, too deeply branded on her psyche for that. Just thinking about it brought a constriction to her throat and tears to her eyes.

The taxi driver and his wife had anointed her with love. Their tender concern and selflessness touched her deeply. *Why*, she thought, *why should they have bothered about me?* They had given her some warm milk and put her to bed, giving up their own bed to her. They had tried to have her stay longer with them, but she had only one obsession — to flee to the West. Any delay in initiating some plan of action would be dangerous.

And this had brought her to Ebenezer Church. She knew nothing of the pastor or the congregation. She had never attended a real worship service. Once she had heard a concert in a church; she had also visited a few cathedrals and this sight-seeing had confirmed for her what she had been taught: the Church was an archaic institution, a relic of the past, a kind of museum. But her Lighter was related to this church and his arranging her escape was her only hope now. His uncle was the custodian. Wouldn't he want to help her, for Werner's sake?

She walked back to the gate and turned in; she went to the church door at the side where she had gone in with Werner. This was where she had found safety and sanctuary with him. It comforted her now as alone she sought refuge here again.

She rang the bell. She waited and waited and there came no answer. Now what to do? There was nowhere else for her to go. She tried the door. It was not locked. She opened it and went in. She would wait for Werner's uncle, or the pastor, or someone to come.

It had been completely dark when she had been here the other time. In the hallway she was confused, not remembering which way Werner had brought her. She tried a door at the end of the corridor. It was a heavy door and it resisted as she pushed against it. She peeked through and saw the lovely stained-glass windows with the morning sun streaming through them. It was a welcoming rhapsody of color. The beauty of it helped to restore some of her confidence. She walked into the church.

"What is it? What can we do for you?" a man's voice said. It startled Lise. She looked around to find its source. She saw no one.

"Hello! Up here!" the voice called again and now it drew Lise's attention to the organ loft. There she saw an elderly man; a feather duster was in his hand.

141

"May I talk to you, please?" she called back. She assumed that the janitor was Werner's uncle. "I'm a friend of Werner Hirn. He's your nephew, isn't he?"

Uncle Klaus hurried down from the balcony. He went up to her excitedly. "Are you the one Werner said was coming?" he asked.

Had Werner told him about her? It was possible. Had he perhaps anticipated that sometime she might come to this church if she needed to get in touch with him?

"I suppose I am," Lise answered.

He invited her to come with him to his room at the back of the church. When she saw it, she remembered the couch where she and Werner had talked. The room felt right, even though she had never seen it in the light of day.

"I know I can talk freely to you if you are Werner Hirn's uncle. I've asked him to help me get to West Berlin."

The old man couldn't conceal his nervousness. "Yes, yes, I know about it. Werner is working on it right now over there. I expect to hear from him soon. I'm waiting for him to tell me what I'm supposed to do next. He said you'd be coming, but . . . ."

There was a long pause. A note of alarm was in his voice as he said, "Maybe there's been some mistake. Did you get the message?"

"What message? I've heard nothing from him."

"Where are the children? There are three children, aren't there?"

"Children?" Lise was getting more confused. The sudden elation she had felt was being diluted with doubt. "I have no children."

He bit his lip as he searched for an answer. He explained that his understanding was that a woman with three children would come to East Berlin after receiving a pre-arranged message. They would have a telephone number to call. He himself had arranged temporary housing for them at Werner's request.

It didn't fit. She knew it and he knew it. This quandary they shared was awkward for both of them.

"I don't know what other arrangements he may be working on," she said, "but he knows I have to cross over and I'm almost sure . . . . I *am* sure . . . . I'm positive he's making some plans to help me. I was supposed to wait for a message, but I couldn't wait. I had to come now. It was now or never."

"And who are you?" the old man asked. "I guess I'd better know that and what connection you have with my nephew."

Lise told him her name and said she'd been with Werner both in Leipzig and here in Berlin. "I'm a friend of his — a very special friend, I think." She was tempted to call herself his fiancée, but she couldn't quite bring herself to that point of presumption. "You can help me, can't you?"

"I wish Werner would come and clear this up himself. It was very clear when he gave me the instructions. I told you what he arranged. I did my part exactly as he said. But maybe his plans changed, and he couldn't get word to me. For some reason he doesn't dare come over any more."

She asked if there wasn't some way to send word to him. Would the pastor of the church be able to help?

"I don't want to involve him in this at all. It's too risky for him. He's already been criticized for being too outspoken. Can't you imagine how they'd use it against the Church if it was discovered that a pastor was smuggling out refugees? No, he mustn't know anything about it."

"You've *got* to help me! I have no other place to go. I can't go back to the apartment where I've been living. I can't return to my work. I'd be arrested. Please give me a place to hide, at least until you hear from Werner. I'm sure he would want you to."

Klaus agreed. "Yes, I guess he would, if what you say is true. Anyway, I have the place all arranged, and I can only hope that Werner wants me to use it for you rather than the woman with the three children. And if they also come . . . ? Well, I hope he sends word to me soon."

143

Having made the decision, and seeing the obvious relief reflected on Lise's face, he smiled reassuringly at her.

"Do you have a suitcase?"

Lise shook her head. "No, I came just like this." She looked down at her dress and realized how incongruous she must seem visiting the church in a low-cut evening dress. She closed her eyes and grimaced as she remembered the occasion for her costume.

They walked the four blocks to the little house that belonged to Frau Wilm. Klaus explained to Lise that until recently this woman had been his housekeeper two days a week. He assured her that Frau Wilm was a faithful church woman who took her Christianity seriously. She was happy only when she could help somebody.

Frau Wilm was all primmed for her guests. She, too, was surprised and troubled that it wasn't the woman with three children she had been expecting. She had even dusted off some old toys and had them ready. But she trusted her good friend Klaus, and accepted the likelihood that there had been some change in the plans. She said that she was lucky to have two bedrooms.

Klaus left Lise in Frau Wilm's care, saying he would be back later to see if he could help with anything. He assured them that he would let them know at once when there was further word from Werner.

Frau Wilm tried to talk to Lise, but Lise was dazed. She found she didn't have words to answer the questions that were asked. Even when her hostess fixed some coffee and sandwiches and encouraged her to have some, Lise just sat there. She was safe now. She knew that. But she couldn't hide forever. What would happen next? This wonderful lady was trying her best to mother her. Lise wanted to respond but she couldn't let herself go. It didn't come naturally to her. Love given demanded love in return and she felt herself barren. She didn't deserve this gentle treatment. She was

144

not worthy of it. She was part of a system, a way of life, that was diabolical and evil. The blackmail tactics of the SSD and the assignment with the Yugoslav had convinced her of that. But even before that, she had known — really, in her heart she had known — that the Soviet-imposed police state was based on fear, hate, expediency, and exploitation. She was a child of that state. She had inherited the fruits of fear and hate and . . . .

Werner, my Lighter! Come to me. Save me from this hell. Take me away. Take me to your heaven!

Frau Wilm had been studying her guest. She saw how Lise was suffering. There was nothing to say to this girl who just stared into space and sat wringing her hands. But when she saw Lise's lips tremble and her body shiver, she knew that she had to do something for her. She sat down beside Lise and put her arm around her.

"Come. I have a bed ready for you. I think you'll feel better after some sleep."

This kindness pierced through the defensive shield to the girl's soul. The response burst forth in a flood of hysteria, uncontrollable sobs and frightening moaning and wailing. The older woman took an afghan from the living room and gently placed it over Lise's shoulders. She led her slowly step by step up the stairs to a bedroom. They sat down together on the edge of the bed. She still had her arm around the weeping girl.

Frau Wilm could do nothing but follow her own motherly intuition. She had comforted her own loved ones many times in the past, but never a stranger like this, an unknown girl who was thus far only an enigma. She started to sing. It had been long ago that she had sung to her own children. But the melody of a beloved old lullaby, and the words, too, came back to her now out of the dim past.

Lullaby, have no fear; guardian angels are near —
Their watch they will keep, while children go to sleep. . . .
Dream the dark night away 'till God's sun brings the day.

Lise listened through the sounds of her own sobbing. Gradually she felt her control returning and she became aware of the presence of the angel sitting with her. The after-spasms continued, but the fog of gloom in her mind began to lift. She turned to offer her hand to Frau Wilm and look into her eyes.

"Thank you. Forgive me for . . . ."

"You're going to sleep now. I'll help you out of your clothes and get one of my nightgowns for you." She left the room and returned shortly with the nightgown, a robe, and a pair of slippers. She poured a glass of water and took a pill out of a little medicine box. "Here. Take this. It will help you sleep."

Lise obeyed. The angel tucked her in and kissed her lightly on the forehead. She pulled the shades and tiptoed out of the room.

Five hours later, as Lise continued to sleep off her emotional exhaustion, Frau Wilm busied herself in her kitchen. She would prepare something she could warm up for the girl when she finally awoke. Or maybe she would sleep around the clock. That would be all right, too. She would need it, not just to regain her strength but to prepare her for the ordeal ahead.

The doorbell rang. She had been expecting Klaus to return. She went to let him in. She hoped he had some news.

On the porch stood a woman and three children.

14

Frau Braun opened the door to Werner. She recognized him immediately. "Good morning! My husband was hoping you'd come. He's in the living room."

The tunneler was busy at a table spread with plans and blueprints. He was examining the markings on a slide rule. He jotted some figures on one of the charts before looking up to greet Werner.

"Hello!" His smile was big and broad, confirming the genuineness of his welcome. "You have good news, I think. Am I right?"

As his answer Werner took out an envelope from his pocket. "Here it is," he said. "In cash — enough for the woman and her three children." He counted it out. In all, six thousand, two hundred and fifty marks.

"Good. I'm glad for you . . . and for them, of course, and for us, too. With the others joining our party, we'll have almost enough to cover the costs. Now, if everything goes according to plan, we'll break through tomorrow night. Not much time, but our team is recruiting help for the final push and I think we'll make it."

This is the time, Werner thought, to talk to him about bringing Lise through the tunnel also. "There's one more person in East Berlin whom I'm hoping to include in your party, but there are a couple of problems."

Herr Braun nodded. "That doesn't surprise me. The next thirty hours will bring us an avalanche of problems. But that's what makes this interesting. You wouldn't believe some of the difficulties we've had this summer — water seepage, mud, lack of money — and fatigue. That's really our biggest problem because the work is so slow and so exhausting. There are times when we are ready to give up. We almost forget why we are working. But then we find a new spurt of energy and things pick up. We dig through these problems as we come to them. Maybe the difficulties you face are something we can help solve."

Werner told him about his friend, Lise, and her desperation to get out. He didn't go into detail about her background and he didn't reveal that she was in the clutches of the secret police. "I hope I can get her out now while we have a way. In another week I'll have to return to my work in Hamburg," Werner said. "I haven't raised the money. But I'm not ready to give up yet. Somehow I think I'll find a way. The really tough problem is how to find her over there and get word to her in time."

"Do you know where she's staying?" Herr Braun asked. "We'll be sending couriers over. Your problem is the same one all our people have. We'll help you, don't worry."

It was good to have him say that but Werner knew it wasn't that simple. He couldn't go over himself, he couldn't send a message to her apartment, he couldn't notify her at the radio station. The only place he could expect to have her found was at the Cosmos Cafe. But how would he dare even alert her to the plan until he knew he could obtain the money?

Another fear was surfacing in his mind: Would it be dangerous to include her in this tunnel plan at all? Might not her trouble with the SSD jeopardize the safety of the others? It wouldn't be strange if they had her under rather close surveillance. Even if they suspected that she might be trying to escape, they might allow her to proceed up to the point of rendezvous for the final tunnel breakthrough, and then, in one

148

bold raid, capture all of them. It wouldn't be the first time the police had used this technique.

He needed some time to ponder this. But time was running out. He needed money. He needed a safe and dependable way to get a message to Lise. But most of all, he needed to be sure himself that it was the right thing to do.

Herr Braun said he could give Werner only until midnight to make the necessary arrangements for the girl.

Where could Frau Spier and her children be picked up by the couriers and be brought to the basement where they would enter the tunnel? Werner didn't know the address of the house where they were waiting. He was hoping and praying they were there. It would be tragic if they had either failed to get the telegram or had experienced difficulty in traveling to East Berlin from Freiberg. Werner suggested that his Uncle Klaus be the contact. The couriers would have to take a message to Ebenezer Church. Werner left, saying he would be back before midnight in any case.

He began driving. He had no destination in mind. He had only his distressing problem to resolve. Driving was a release from the frustration of indecision. It was action . . . motion . . . progress. The traffic crowding him and the stop lights halting him and even the sewer excavations deflecting him created a kinetic tempo for his thoughts. The route of his drive was wholly improvised. He needed to think . . . think . . . think.

Twenty-five hundred marks! That wasn't so much. But if you didn't have it, it could just as well be a million. Twenty-five hundred, though, might actually be obtainable if he could only think of how and where and from whom. The Jewish doctor? Frau Dreitlein had had no difficulty. No, he couldn't go back there. That was a special case and to ask for more would merely spoil the splendid poetic justice of the doctor's redemptory gesture.

Could he get it from his office? Would they give him a salary advance? No. No. He knew that employers never appreciate requests like that. It's poor policy for both parties.

A bank wouldn't make a loan for this. He could hardly use Lise as collateral. Who would be interested in helping an ex-Party activist, an ex-radio propagandist, and an ex-informer for the SSD? The Americans? They had their military intelligence and the CIA in Berlin. Wouldn't they pay something to get her story? He didn't know any American officials — Fritz worked for them at the station but he was a German, a Berliner, and was just an employee. But he'd know whom to contact, wouldn't he? Werner thought about it hopefully for a few minutes. No. He really didn't want to make this an incident, even a tiny incident, in the cold war by involving Lise officially with any government. And not the West Berlin city government, either. He tried to remember what he had heard about refugee organizations. Did they have funds for an emergency like this? How could he find out about them?

As he was driving along, he looked at the traffic and the streets and buildings, but he really didn't see them except as a moving background for the drama being rehearsed in his mind. At an intersection where he had to wait for the light to change he glanced across the street. All that met his eyes was an advertising sign with banners flying above a row of automobiles in a parking lot. Then he joined the onrush of traffic urging him along. After a moment, the subliminal exposure of the sight of those cars standing in the lot finally registered in his conscious mind: That sign! It said USED CARS BOUGHT AND SOLD. He could sell his car! It would bring more than the twenty-five hundred marks he would need. A Volkswagen, new and in good shape like this one, would always be redeemable for cash. He might take a loss in selling it outright but it would bring him the money in a hurry.

The stimulation of this possibility as the solution of one of his major problems cleared his mind. He noticed now where he was. In his aimless cruising through the streets of Berlin, he had drifted over near the Wall. There it was at the end of this street.

Bernauerstrasse. Here the Wall had produced its most infamous political, geographical, and human aberration. For more than a mile the Wall was mortised together by buildings — houses, apartments, factories, churches. Front doors and windows had been sealed against the climate of freedom on Bernauerstrasse. Most of the occupants had been cleared from the structures and now only Vopos could occasionally be seen standing guard in the empty rooms.

Werner passed several points that had become shrines for the people of West Berlin. Floral wreathes still marked the spot where Olga Segler jumped to her death from that third-floor window above . . . where Berndt Lunser was seized and killed as he was about to leap to safety . . . . Ida Siekmann . . . . Rolf Urban. On one building someone had painted in large letters the one word: MURDER.

He drove by the famous church whose front door was cemented over, thereby cutting off the majority of the congregation. The irony of the church's name did not escape him: The Church of the Reconciliation!

Over that wall, he thought, *Lise waits. I am her only hope. Would I ever forgive myself if I failed her and left her over there to be devoured? But if I did try and then had the months of preparations for escape for others meet tragedy because of her, could I live with that on my conscience for life?*

He stopped and parked his car. He walked over to the Wall. It rose higher than his head and was topped with the barbed wire of a concentration camp. A platform had been built to allow tourists to look over to the other side. He climbed up. His view was blocked by huge wooden screens that had been erected on the other side. Nevertheless, Werner stood there a moment. *Where was Lise in that massive prison compound? Was she waiting, even at this moment,*

151

*for her deliverer? Was she praying — it wasn't impossible
that she might be — for salvation?*

He continued his tour of inspection on a course parallel to
the Wall. Near Checkpoint Charlie was the grim memorial
to Peter Fechter, whose dying gasps were heard around the
world. At Friedrichstrasse there was the usual line of waiting cars with their foreign license plates. He parked nearby.

From one of the waiting vehicles, a Volkswagen Microbus,
a family group emerged. The father remained at the wheel
to inch his way along in the line toward the checkpoint while
the mother went with two teen-age boys over to the sidewalk and crossed in front of Werner. He heard them speaking
English.

"I think we can go right in, Mom," one of the boys said.
"Nobody's selling tickets." He indicated the open door of
Checkpoint Charlie Presspoint, an abandoned shop where a
display of pictures, maps, and news clippings about the Wall
was housed as a gallery for tourists. They went in.

Werner followed. He watched them. The only other visitors looking at the exhibit were leaving. The boys glanced at
each item quickly and soon were at the other end. The
mother took the time, however, to read the news accounts below the headlines. Werner walked over to her. "Terrible,
isn't it?" he said to her in English.

"Yes, really shocking," she answered. "You must actually
see it to understand it, I think. We saw this on television
back home at the time of President Kennedy's visit. When
we planned our trip, this was the one thing we most wanted
to see."

He hoped he could talk more to her. But as a stranger he
didn't want to appear presumptuous. He waited.

"Is it dangerous to go over to East Berlin?" she asked.

"Not for Americans."

"We were told we could take our car over. I hope it will
be all right."

He smiled. "I'm sure it will be. I wish I could go, but I

can't. My girl friend is over there but I can't go over to see her any more." He didn't explain it further.

"Come on, Mom, we'd better get back to the car." The boys were going out the door.

"Would you . . . would you be willing to do something for me today over in East Berlin?" Yes, it was worth the chance at least to try.

"Well, that depends . . . . What sort of thing?"

He replied, "I have a very important message that must reach my fiancée today. I'm not allowed to take it to her myself. I know where she will be — at the Cosmos Cafe on Karl Marx Allee. Would you be willing to deliver a note to her for me?"

"Oh, you'd better talk to my husband about that. He's out in the car. Why don't you ask him?"

Werner had hoped it wouldn't have to be that complicated. Nevertheless, he had started this and might as well pursue it. They went out and noticed immediately that not much forward progress had been made. Werner waited on the sidewalk while the woman went over to the car, got in, and talked to her husband. They all looked over at Werner and then discussed the situation among themselves some more. The woman beckoned to him to come over.

Werner introduced himself to the driver and apologized for the strange request he had made. But he repeated that it was urgent. The boys in back, at their father's suggestion, opened the door and Werner was asked to sit in the car and talk it over. The man introduced himself as an American college professor. He was urbane and knowledgeable and spoke in German. This allowed Werner to speak freely. He told the man that his fiancée would be waiting at the Cosmos Cafe for a message from him and that it contained instructions for an escape route for her that he had planned.

The man agreed. Desperately, Werner tried to describe her. He wouldn't know where she would be sitting, or what she would be wearing. Then he remembered his own rendezvous with her there and the waiter who helped him find her. He described the waiter — the only one he had seen at the Cosmos; the others were waitresses. Werner suggested that they give him a tip and ask if he could show them to Fräulein Liselotte Lehman's table. That was the best he could do.

He scribbled out a short note: *Everything is set. See my uncle at Ebenezer Church. I am waiting for you. Your Lighter.* Then before folding the note, he added, *God keep you!*

He waited at the Presspoint until he saw the car with the Americans disappear behind the Wall.

15

LISE WAS NOT WAITING AT THE COSMOS CAFE. SINCE EARLY
afternoon she had been lying asleep in an upstairs bedroom in
the home of Frau Wilm. It was a merciful sleep for the
frightened girl whose emotional reserve had been so completely debilitated. In her state of shock, sleep had been induced
not so much by the mild sedative she had been given; rather,
it had come as the narcotic result of a "truth serum" that had
exposed her naked soul.

Her hours of deep unconsciousness gradually slid into the
sweet torpor of *Dämmerschlaf,* the anesthetized twilight where
pain and the memory of pain are suspended. It was dark.
But time didn't matter. Deadlines and pressures and schedule
anxieties had been nullified by the clemency of slumber.

Nor did any sound disturb her or cause her to question its
source and significance — the sound of voices being modulated
against the whimpering of a child. The buoyancy of her sleep
lifted Lise back to moments of her own childhood, moments
of make-believe . . . discovery . . . gaiety . . . song . . . belonging! But as her waking came, it ushered in memories of dis-
tant pain, of fatherlessness . . . of maternal remoteness . . . of
study and form and slogans and flags and marching . . . and
pledges and disciplines for the Party, the Party, the Party.
That sound? The sound . . . the sound of crying . . . the crying
of a child was not on her dream track at all! It was real. A
real child. Real crying. In the next room!

"Ilse, Ilse, listen to me! Mommy's here. I'm watching you. Everything will be all right."

Lise listened.

"I know, Ilse, darling, I know. We left so suddenly. You didn't have time to say good-by to any of your friends. But it's better this way. We're on a big adventure. I can't tell you exactly what will happen. It's like a trip to a place we've never been before. It will be fun discovering things along the way."

The crying continued. Was Lise still dreaming? No, she was very much awake now and the sounds and the voices she heard were coming from the next bedroom in this house.

"But I don't want to go on the trip. I'm afraid. Helmut said that we'll have to go over the Wall and I'm afraid to. I heard about the people who try to go over the Wall. There are guns and shooting and people get killed and I don't want that to happen to us. Can't we go home again? I want to go home. I can't help it that I'm afraid. I am —"

"Ilse, dearest, I know you can't help it. But there *is* help for fear. You know that. We've been afraid before. I've been afraid. I could cry now, too, if I let myself. But I know that there is help for frightened people. For me and for you and for all who need it. Our Lord has promised that. We know He answers our prayers. *This* is an answer to prayer — our being here. So, why shouldn't He take away our fear if we ask Him to?"

The crying subsided. The silence was punctuated only by an occasional sob. Lise put her feet on the floor. She tiptoed to the open door.

"Dear Heavenly Father, we thank You for answering our prayers. We thank You for the courage You give us to face the new adventures You set before us. Give us faith to believe in You, to accept what You have provided for us. Fill our hearts with new hope for living and for what is prepared for us beyond life. And warm us with Your love, so that we also can love all persons — even those who cause us pain.

156

Please, dear Lord, in Your good time, have the bad and wicked Wall removed. Give this world peace through the Prince of Peace. We ask — Ilse and Helmut and Ursula and I — that You will protect us from harm and danger on our trip, and bring us safely to the other side . . . if it be Your will. We pray in Jesus' name, Amen."

"Our Father, who art in heaven. . . ." Lise heard other voices joining in. She stood rigid by the door.

When she saw the light in the next room go out, she slipped on the robe Frau Wilm had left for her and quietly crossed over to the stairs and slowly descended. From the bottom step she saw in the dim glow of a shaded lamp that Frau Wilm was asleep on the divan. She turned and walked up the stairs again. At the top stood Frau Spier.

"Hello," she whispered to Lise. "I'm sorry if my children awakened you."

"No, no. I had slept too long, anyway." Lise invited her into her bedroom. She turned on the bed lamp.

"Frau Wilm told us about you," the widow said after she had introduced herself. "How do you feel?"

Lise responded with a wan smile. "Much better, thanks." Then she realized that she had a large room to herself, and Frau Spier and her three children were all in one room. "Let a couple of the children have my bed," she suggested.

"Thank you, but they're almost asleep now."

"But you — you haven't slept. You take my bed."

"We'll see. Perhaps I can share it with you. But I don't expect to sleep much tonight. Tomorrow will be such an exciting day."

"I heard you talking to your child," Lise admitted with embarrassment. "There was something about a trip, wasn't there?"

Frau Spier looked at her curiously. "But surely you know? Then again, maybe you don't. You . . . you didn't know about our coming, did you? Of course! How could you?"

"I don't understand."

157

"We expect word tomorrow about going to the West — to West Berlin."

Then it dawned on Lise. "You're the woman with three children — the ones the man from the church was expecting! How did you get here?"

"We came by train from Freiberg."

Freiberg . . . Freiberg! It became clear to her now. Werner had needed a visa for Freiberg. He had told his uncle that a woman with three children was coming. These arrangements, this plan — they weren't for her at all.

"What's the matter?" Frau Spier had noticed the horrified look on Lise's face.

Lise couldn't answer. The awful nightmare was returning. The pain of her loneliness, her hopelessness, her fear was flooding upon her again.

"Did I say something wrong?"

Lise looked at her through tears. "No, of course not. Do you know who Werner Hirn is?"

"Why, yes. I certainly do. He came to see me in Freiberg. He is helping my mother to get us out. We expect to learn more about it tomorrow. Perhaps he'll come to see us here."

"He won't!" Lise blurted it out. "He can't!"

Surprise and dismay covered the widow's countenance. "You haven't told me how *you* happen to know Werner Hirn," she said.

Lise told her the whole story. In a flood of words she reconstructed the complete history of their relationship: the chance meetings in Berlin, the trip to Leipzig, the reunion in Berlin, and her pleading with Werner to rescue her, to help her escape to West Berlin.

"Why do you have to leave? Are you in trouble?"

It was so complicated. How could this woman appreciate Lise's trouble? Should she tell her of her Communist background, of her service to the Party with the East Berlin radio? Should she tell her that the Stasi was blackmailing her and waiting now to arrest her because she defaulted on her assignment to be their agent?

"Trouble? Yes, I'm in trouble. I'm wanted by the police. But that's only the beginning of my trouble. Or maybe it will be the end of it, I don't know. I don't know anything any more. I'm terribly confused and sick and weary and frightened. Yes, I'm really frightened. Worse fear than your child had. You see, I know what can happen to me. And it's worse than any child's imagination could make it."

She wanted to cry. But there wasn't even strength for that.

"But the answer for you is the same as it was for her," Frau Spier said softly. "There is help for fear. The courage that God gives us through Christ. He has promised it. He provides it."

Lise shook her head. "I wish I could believe that. But all my life I've been taught . . . ." She stopped. Where could this lead? It couldn't help her escape her problems. They would still have to be faced. She didn't have the strength to discuss religion. And yet she was afraid and this woman wasn't. The why of it gnawed at her.

"Prove to me that God exists!" Lise almost flung the challenge at her. "Give me just one shred of evidence — scientific evidence — that your God is real and that he does all those things you told your child he promises and that you prayed for."

"I can't give you evidence. God doesn't need proof. He *is*, that's all. If we could measure Him and examine Him and satisfy ourselves that our intellects can contain Him, we wouldn't need faith. And faith is what I live by."

"Faith? What is faith?"

" 'Faith is the substance of things hoped for, the evidence of things not seen. . . .' That's the only definition I have. It's from the Bible."

"And you really believe that God exists and that he helps you?"

159

"Yes, I couldn't live if I —" She stopped. She realized then that she was talking with a person who was spiritually barren. But she also recognized there a hunger and a need. "I can only tell you what I know — what I have experienced. It may not be anything that you can understand. But it's real and precious to me. That's all I can say . . . that's all the evidence I have."

Lise looked at her long and thoughtfully. "What would you do if you were me . . . now?"

"What do you mean?"

"If you knew that your hopes for rescue were all crushed, if you knew you had to go out into the city of East Berlin tomorrow and be tracked down by the secret police and arrested and likely spend the next years — five or ten or more — in prison? What would you do?"

Frau Spier looked at Lise searchingly. "I don't know. I really don't. But I would try not to give up hope for rescue."

"But he isn't interested in me! It's you he's saving."

"How can you be so sure? Do you know what he's doing now? Why, he may be making plans for you this very minute. He may be trying to reach you. He may have wonderful news for you."

"But there's no way for me to reach him."

"You could pray."

"I can't pray."

"Then I'll pray for you."

16

DOWN AT THE MOUTH OF THE TUNNEL, FIFTEEN FEET UNDER-ground, the freshly mined dirt had a peculiar smell. Its odor was almost spicy, as if the secrets of forgotten centuries had been released in this exhumation of compressed decay.

Werner was stripped to the waist and his muscles rebelled against the heaviness of the sodden soil he lifted from the conveyer cart and poured into the wheelbarrow. He rolled the full load over planks down the basement passageway to a room at the end, the last of seven cellar chambers appropriated by the tunnel team for storing the dirt.

Knowing that extra manpower was needed for the final push, Werner had volunteered. Once he had dispatched the message to Lise with the American tourists and had ex-changed his car for cash, Werner had only to worry and wait. He had risked the deposit for Lise's passage with the full knowledge that it couldn't be refunded if she failed to appear. He wanted to be doing something that would keep him occupied and allow him to participate physically in the rescue effort.

Herr Braun had led him to the factory building whose large basement the team had rented near the Wall in West Berlin. Nothing on the outside had revealed the feverish activity going on in the cellar below the old brick building. It had been dark when Herr Braun turned the key in a side door that led to an ordinary flight of stairs going down.

The first room had been bare except for a clothesline on which hung mud-starched work clothes. Hooks along the wall had held street clothing, white shirts, sweaters, and trousers belonging to the tunnel team. Werner had been introduced to them in the next room. Several others had been at the opposite end of the tunnel. Nearly all of them were students at the Free University. Informality ruled among the team and only first names or nicknames were used. Herr Braun was Falcon. Werner had been welcomed by Günther, Little Fox, Hans, Kaj, and also by Jaeger, Dieter, and General.

What he had expected the tunnel to be like, Werner didn't know, but certainly nothing as ambitious and complicated as this. He had been surprised at the variety of equipment and mechanical gear spread around on the floor and in the shadowy corners and on the brick basement walls: electrical panels with lines running to a water pump and an air compressor and a motorized windlass. According to Hans, the latter machine had proved indispensable in pulling the dirt cart along the steel track. Load after load from deep within the tunnel had come out, accummulating into tons and tons of earth.

Most fascinating to Werner had been the long tunnel shaft itself. He had been allowed to crawl into it a part of the way toward the East on his hands and knees. A long string of light bulbs stretched ahead to a narrow point where the tunnel turned. The cavity was uncomfortably confining — only three feet high and three feet wide. Werner had been weary of crawling after passing only about a dozen of the wooden timber supports that shored the sides and top. For those escaping it would be a grim journey, burrowing along for almost six hundred feet, over half of that under the death strip on the East side, and then under the Wall itself. After that, with the coveted goal in sight, the remaining distance would be less formidable.

Werner had heard the rumble of cars and trucks and trams on the street above him. By holding very still he had also been able to hear the clicking of a woman's heels on the coblestones overhead. If sound from above could be transmitted down to them in the tunnel, would not passers-by overhead be able to hear the digging sounds from below? With Vopos patrolling fifteen feet above them on the East side, the detection of any suspicious noises could be disastrous.

Finally, when Werner had hauled away the last cart-load of dirt, word was flashed back that the diggers at the far end had reached the stone foundation wall of the terminal target building. The team had a hurried conference. As Werner listened, he sat down on a cot. He was out of breath from his exertions and his body was slimy with sweat and dirt.

The diggers with their shovels were called back. Falcon and Jaeger would take over because they had had the most experience in the delicate task of chipping away the mortar with chisels and drills. It would take them several hours to loosen the stones and penetrate the basement room on the other side.

The big question that would come as the climax of their many weeks of work was this: What would they find on the other side? If the scouts over there had been right in their initial assessment of that East Berlin building as reasonably safe, they could expect to bore into an empty room. But they never knew. Other tunnelers had broken through basements over there only to find themselves staring into the gun barrels of waiting police. Falcon and Jaeger armed themselves with pistols and submachine guns and disappeared down the tunnel.

It was Saturday, 3 p.m. The first refugee was scheduled to break through at 6 p.m. There was no more that Werner could do. He would have time to change his clothes, go home to Clayallee, and give his mother and Frau Dreitlein a progress report and take a bath. But he didn't really want to leave the scene so close to the time of climax. He wanted to be right here, ready to welcome Frau Spier and her family *if* they came and to embrace Lise *if* she came.

Little Fox suggested he lie down on the cot and have a nap. Werner didn't expect to sleep. The suspense had tightened his nerves. His body, however, sagged under the lingering burden of the work he had done. He lay down.

Would they come? If only he had met Falcon and his team earlier! He could have plotted the strategy of communication and rendezvous in East Berlin much more efficiently. It had all been so dangerously improvised at the last minute that anything could go wrong. If the suspicions of the SSD had not been provoked, he could be over there this minute personally delivering his charges to the tunnel entrance. A sudden thought came to him. Should he hazard another crossing anyway, even at this eleventh hour? He could at least find out from Uncle Klaus if Lise had come and if everything was set for the Spier family. Should he? No. It would be foolhardy. He had had warning enough. It might take him two hours to go through the checkpoint on a Saturday afternoon. And he could be arrested. Others had, for lesser reasons. No. No. He had to wait here and hope.

And pray? Was it right to call upon God in a moment of anxiety like this and expect Him to use His supernatural powers to correct the errors and oversights of men? Was God a kind of superman to be hired as an insurance against the chances of failure? Anyway, wasn't the die already cast? Hadn't the Spiers and Lise either arrived by now at the rendezvous point or not? Could his praying change anything?

Werner was surprised at his own cynicism and doubt. There had been a time when, in childlike trust, he had laid out the entire collection of his problems before an all-powerful, all-knowing, all-seeing God and expected solutions to come like magic. Nevertheless, he felt the need, as he lay waiting in the subterranean sanctuary of these catacombs, to pray for God's blessing on today's encounter with destiny.

He had learned in catechism class that it was legitimate to pray for any good thing as long as the petition was accompanied by "if it be Thy will." *Thy will be done . . . .*

164

For Lise . . . for him . . . for Widow Spier . . . for Jaeger and Falcon and Little Fox. How would he ever know if his prayer had been answered? *Deliver us from evil . . . .* No problem there. The possibilities for evil were omnipresent. He could at least plead the cause of deliverance for those waiting behind the Wall — for those who might come tonight, for those who would remain. *And deliver me from evil, too . . . .*

He awoke to find Little Fox shaking him. "It's time," he said. "The first ones will be coming through in a few minutes."

Werner jumped up. He shook his head and rubbed his eyes. Ooooh! His muscles and joints protested. "Okay . . . okay. What should I do?"

Little Fox told him he was supposed to be one of the relay sentinels inside the tunnel. His assignment was to assist and hurry the adults along and carry any baby or small child to the next man. He gave him a shoulder holster and a pistol. "Let's hope you don't need this," he said with a wry smile.

Someone offered Werner a cup of hot coffee. It helped to clear his mind. Then he crawled forward into the tunnel to his assigned place.

He heard some loud whispers from up ahead. He saw the contorted shadows of a bulky form approaching his station. These alerted Werner to the first consignment of human cargo arriving on this conveyer belt to freedom. It was a woman. Her head was bent and he couldn't see her face. As she passed, she turned to give him a quick smile.

"Not far left," he whispered. "Can you make it all right?"

"If my knees hold out. Raw and bleeding. But you won't hear me complaining."

And then she was gone. Who was it? Some bride on her way to her wedding? There was a wait before the next body appeared. Who would this be? What if it were

165

— No. It was a child. Behind her crawled a man. A father coaxing his child to another world.

Ferrying the babes in arms was difficult. There were about six of them at intervals. Crawling with them was almost impossible. Werner tried waddling from a squatting position. The last few yards to the next relay point he walked on his knees. Awkward and painful though it was, the sensation of holding a baby in his arms down there and having a small share in giving the child transport to a new life filled him with transcendent wonder.

The bare bulbs strung along the tunnel gave a weird light tangled with shadows. He couldn't see clearly enough to recognize any of those who came groveling along like animals in the fantastic underground parade. There wasn't time to talk with them either. He suspected that one of the women who wormed her way past him could have been Frau Spier. None of them, so far, had been Lise — he was sure of that.

Finally, the word was passed from sentry to sentry: "That's it. The whole group. Twenty. Let's join them!"

The next moments were a nightmare of bewilderment. The rescue had been completed. Victory! All safe. No screams. No shooting. No hellish gun battles in the bowels of the earth. Now, faster than the fugitives, the ushers themselves were being prodded through the intestines of Berlin. With a kind of peristaltic desperation, they pushed their way out.

A cavern full of chaos awaited them — crying infants being cuddled and comforted. Crying lovers reunited. Ragged stockings with huge gaping holes at the knees being ripped off bleeding legs. Children sitting on stones, disappointed in the heaven they had been promised, patiently praying for release from this purgatory. Men washing the mud gloves from their hands. Women dunking their shoes in the same water.

Werner went from one group to another, searching forms and faces. *Lise . . . Lise, where are you? Did you come?*

166

That woman over there, combing a little girl's hair. Frau Spier! Oh, thank God.

He touched her shoulder. "Frau Spier?"

She turned instantly to him. "Yes, yes, but who . . . who are you?"

"Hirn. Werner Hirn."

She looked at him, disbelieving. How could she have recognized him in his mask of dirt and grime? Then she smiled in happy recognition with tears choking her laughter, and threw her arms around him.

"Children, this is Herr Hirn. We owe him very, very much." She introduced Ursula, Helmut, and Ilse.

"Your grandmother is waiting for you," he said to them. "She has a big dinner ready. You'll be there very soon."

Then he turned to Frau Spier. "Excuse me, please. I'll be with you in just a moment. There's someone else I'm looking for."

He hurried away. Frau Spier watched him go and then buried her face in her hands.

After a moment she turned to her children and said, "Wait right here. I'll be back in a minute."

Werner found Falcon. "Are you sure that's all? She didn't come. She isn't here. Is the tunnel still open?"

Herr Braun took Werner's arm. "I was there. No one else came. We took them all. Sorry. Maybe there'll be another chance if the tunnel isn't discovered."

Werner leaned down to look into the empty artery. The string of lights snaked down the deep eternity that yawned before him.

"She's not coming." The voice was behind him.

Werner looked up into the eyes of Frau Spier. "What did you say?"

"You're looking for Lise Lehman. I know. I was with her last night."

"Last night? *Why didn't you bring her with you?*"

She shook her head. She couldn't find the words.

"Why? Why? What happened?"

Frau Spier opened her purse. She looked at Werner. "I talked to her last night. She didn't know you had made any plans for her. This morning when I awoke she was gone. She left this for you." Frau Spier handed him an envelope.

Werner just stared at it. Frau Spier kissed him on the cheek and left him alone with the letter.

> *Dear, dear Lighter — When you get this, I will be somewhere behind the Wall starting to rebuild my life. Foolishly, in my fear, I thought I could flee from myself. If only I could transfer to another world, I could be someone else. No more me. It was a delicious thought, tempting. It would solve all my problems.*
>
> *Yesterday morning I went to Ebenezer Church. I talked to your uncle. For a few moments when he thought I was Frau Spier, he talked about your plans to rescue me. It was like a miracle, but it turned out to be a cruel coincidence. Frau Spier came after all — to the same place where I had already stolen her bed. Then I knew that it was she, not I, for whom you had made the arrangements.*
>
> *I've thought about us. Probably we'll never meet again. I cry as I think of it. Was it love that passed between us? It might have come to that. But more than a wall is separating us.*
>
> *I've thought about you. You were generous and thoughtful and patient and understanding. I needed all of that — almost demanded it of you, I guess. Thank you for not refusing. I'll always be thankful to you. But I was selfish and thought only of myself, never of you. What did you need? What will you need? Perhaps it's best that it stops here. If you had been able to bring me over there — and I still think you tried — what freedom would that have given you to choose me or not?*
>
> *Maybe you won't understand what I'm going to tell you. I'm not sure I completely understand it myself. It began with you, my Lighter. You were that to me. You brought a little light into the darkness of my mind . . . enough to show me who I might really be. And then I was blinded! I thought I would never see again. The acid of hate blurred and burned and obscured reality. I hated myself. I hated*

168

you. I hated even your God that I had told myself was only a phantom.

But then, at the very extremity of my feeble vision, the miracle came. Light. Dim and refracted, yes. But there in my dark desperation, some human angels surrounded me. They gave me love, and with it hope and light.

I see now that I belong here, not there. I don't know what will happen. They will not have love gifts for me. No light to offer. Prisons can be very dark.

But someone, one of the Angels of Light, taught me how not to be afraid. I tried it. I don't know yet if this is really the answer. At least as I write this I'm not afraid any more.

It's like going on a long trip through the darkness. Those who have lights can lead the way. Perhaps even Lise — sometime — can be a Lighter.

You, dear one, don't worry about me. Go back to Hamburg happily, knowing that your light still shines over here behind the Wall.

— Lise

P.S. I'm taking a little book that belongs to Frau Spier. I think she'd want me to have it. Buy her another one over there, will you?